THE CORPSE CLUE
THE COMPLETE CASES OF MORTON
& McGARVEY, VOLUME 1

THE CORPSE CLUE
THE COMPLETE CASES OF
MORTON & McGARVEY, VOLUME 1

DONALD BARR CHIDSEY

ILLUSTRATED BY
JOHN FLEMING GOULD

COVER BY
WALTER BAUMHOFER

POPULAR PUBLICATIONS · 2022

TABLE OF CONTENTS

PRIZE BULL 1

MURDER BY PROXY 33

THE CORPSE CLUE 73

THE CARRION CLUE 127

THE SCAR CLUE 173

Young McGarvey admitted he wasn't very smart and his sidekick, Morton, was inclined to agree. In fact the older officer would never have taken on the big blundering kid for a partner if the lad's father hadn't been his best friend. But murder, it seems, can do wonders toward turning even the callowest calf of a copper into a—

PRIZE BULL

THE HOUSE WAS a big one, very grand and a show place even in Brickell Avenue. It was ablaze with light, and loud with syncopated music.

"They don't seem to be worrying much about it, whatever it is," McGarvey complained. He was young, and this was his first night as a detective. He had been hoping for a good assault case, at least.

"Swell affair," Morton grunted. "This is the Wetmore dump. You know—Wetmore Cough Drops."

There was a patrol sedan at the front entrance, and McGarvey parked close behind it. A Negro in a white coat, who carried a folded umbrella, offered to put the car elsewhere.

"You leave it right here!" McGarvey shouted—and Morton winced.

Two uniformed cops and a man in full evening dress were on the veranda. The cops were unfeignedly glad to see Morton and McGarvey.

"These fellas'll talk to you. We don't know anything except that we got a radio call to stop here and see who yelled for help," they said.

"Utter nonsense! My wife and I are entertaining, and we don't want policemen running all over the estate!" Wetmore shouted.

McGarvey barged into the group. "Too bad," he boomed,

*"Better come in
and say hello,"
Morton invited*

glaring at the cough-drop king. William T. Wetmore was small and flabby, and extraordinarily pale. His features seemed as unsubstantial and almost as colorless as a *charlotte russe*. Morton was tempted to stick a finger into one of the cheeks, to see whether it would leave a hole.

"If you don't want cops, why did somebody call us?" Morton asked.

"You're crazy! Nobody called you!"

"Yeah? Well, some woman yelled for police headquarters, and then she made a gurgling sound in her tonsils— and hung up. The operator tried to get her back but the line was dead," the detective retorted.

"Absolute nonsense! The operator must have made a mistake."

"Well, this is Hill, Two-four-four-six-four, ain't it?" Mort asked.

"Yes, that's my number, but I'm sure nobody called any such message from here. Either my wife or myself, or else our son, has been within a few feet of that instrument every minute for the past two hours or more. Plenty of others have too. You can see it through the glass here," Wetmore pointed out.

Yes, the telephone was in full view; and guests, all unaware of the fuss on the veranda drifted back and forth past it. An orchestra was playing. On the right, people were dancing, and on the left of the entrance hall they were standing in groups, talking, drinking.

"It must be some mistake. I don't want my guests disturbed and—"

"We won't disturb them." Morton, irritated by his new partner's noisiness, opened the door, pushed through, picked up the telephone. No buzzing, no humming. "It's dead all right," he said sadly.

A BUTLER WAS informing William Wetmore that he couldn't seem to find William Wetmore, Jr. The host made an impatient gesture.

"He must be around somewhere! I want him to talk to these men. Mrs. Wetmore needs me inside. Did you try upstairs? I saw him go up there a little while ago."

Morton said to the butler: "Wait a minute." To Wetmore he said: "Maybe there's an extension upstairs, eh?"

Wetmore snapped his fingers. "Of course! I'd forgotten all about it, in the excitement. There's one in my own bedroom—in the back of the house."

The butler went first, to guide them; McGarvey, a close second, was trying to look grim and forbidding. Wetmore cast a final glance around the main hall, like a man who fears a tongue-lashing from his wife; and Morton—slow and patient Morton—plodded along in the rear. Music swirled up after them.

Downstairs everybody seemed to be having a good time. Wonderful parties the Wetmores gave. They had lots of money, and didn't care how they spent it. Wetmore, Jr., an only child, had been burning up the local night clubs. The magnate's wife was a notorious plunger in the gambling rooms. Wetmore himself didn't do much except sign checks, but he did that well and often.

"Should be an upstairs maid here," he grumbled. "We had her here to take care of the wraps."

The rear of the mansion faced Biscayne Bay, and the master's bedroom was there. McGarvey pushed ahead of the butler and threw open the door. For an instant he stood in the threshold, his bulk obstructing the view. "Fer Gawd's sake," he said slowly. Then he sprang into the room.

Morton snarled from the doorway: "Don't move it! That's in a funny position, and I don't want it moved till we get pictures!"

McGarvey announced over a shoulder that he hadn't been born yesterday—all he was trying to do was find out if she was dead.

She was dead all right. Morton knew this at a glance. Wetmore knew it too, and sat down suddenly, looking as though he were about to be sick.

"My God," he muttered, "the whole party will be spoiled!"

"Shame," growled McGarvey.

She had been pretty—a brunette, small, about twenty-three, dressed in a black uniform. Her face was dark purple, and her eyes, wide open, bulged hideously. She lay on her back. A gayly figured sport scarf was tied very tight around her neck, from behind. There were five or six slashes in her side just under the left armpit, and the rug below these was wet with blood.

"This that upstairs maid you were talking about?"

Wetmore seemed not to have heard, but the butler nodded.

Morton knelt beside McGarvey. Gingerly he pressed a forefinger into the bloodstain on the rug, and then he withdrew the finger and stared at its tip. He looked as though he were about to sniff it, but didn't. Instead he poked carefully at the slashes in the dress.

McGARVEY WATCHED HIM sidewise, awed. He was very eager to appear experienced, a real detective, but he knew as well as everybody else on the Miami force, that sheer sentimentality had been the reason for his promotion from harness. His father, killed in a recent gun battle, had been Morton's partner for many years, and everybody had liked him. Young McGarvey was lucky, and he knew it, and it made him nervous—which in turn made him loud-mouthed, violent. His greatest luck, he thought, was getting this assignment as Morton's sidekick. Morton was the best detective in Florida—the best in the world, if you asked young McGarvey. Morton'd been his hero for years.

"Some of these go right through and some don't,"

Morton mused, "but even the ones that do ain't very deep. Funny."

"She was choked to death! Garroted!"

"Sure." Morton pushed his finger into the bloodstain again, and again he stared morosely at it. "There's an awful lot of this stuff—"

McGarvey had withdrawn a note from one of the uniform pockets. It was brief, and it made him blush—but it gave him something to do, something to bluster about.

"This girl's name was Ellen?"

"That's right," Wetmore said. "Ellen Wilcox."

"You ever fool around with her?"

"Of course not! I resent that question! What right have you to—"

"All right then. Did she ever make any passes at you?"

Wetmore shrugged. "I don't like to talk ill of the dead, but she was rather—well, flirtatious. At least she was when she first came to us, about two months ago. I gave her to understand that I didn't approve of such conduct."

"Just the same, you didn't mind writing her hot letters, huh?"

"See here! I won't stand for any such remarks!"

"Your first name's William, ain't it?" McGarvey thrust the note under Wetmore's nose. "Well, is that your handwriting or ain't it?"

Wetmore's eyes grew very large, and he seemed to rush to the edge of sickness all over again. Once more he sat down.

"That—that's not my handwriting. No."

"I hope you're telling the truth," McGarvey stormed, "because it's going to be easy to check."

Morton, studying the note, asked quietly: "Mr. Wetmore, didn't I hear you say you saw your son come upstairs a little while ago?"

"Why, I—I—did I say that?"

"You did. And his first name's William too, isn't it?"

McGarvey started for the door. "Hell! I never thought of that!" He shook the butler. "Come on, James. You point this kid out to me."

"And first," Morton called, "make sure you tell the boys out front that nobody leaves the place. Tell one of 'em to take the car and run down to the nearest phone and get the headquarters gang here." He sighed, returning to his survey of the room. "Looks like an all-night job," he told nobody in particular.

THE TELEPHONE WAS a French type instrument, on a little table near the bed. It was dead, like the instrument downstairs. French windows opened upon a large balcony, more like an upstairs veranda. Morton locked the hall door, and beckoned to the palpitating millionaire.

"Don't want anybody to come rubbering in here," he explained. "You better come along with me, huh? Show me around out back." They went out.

The balcony was roofed by awnings, and the floor was dry. There were a few pieces of wicker furniture. At a corner of the house, within easy reach, an electric wire had been hacked loose.

"There's what happened to the phone, anyway."

An outside stairway, independent of the house itself, led to the garden. With a flashlight, Morton found a few footprints, which he was able to follow as far as a concrete walk leading back to the garages. The large concrete apron in front of the garages, and a stretch of concrete drive-way crowded with the cars of guests, made further search impractical for the present.

"How come there are no chauffeurs hanging around out here?"

"We asked them into the kitchen when the shower started," Wetmore replied.

Morton returned to the footprints. They led away from the balcony stairs. They were blurred, but apparently small, narrow. The rain, the first in many weeks, had been brief, and the ground was still hard. Morton, himself, weighed one seventy, yet his own feet left no lasting prints in this grass. Moreover, the mark of the heel was plain, emphatic. A man running does not ordinarily make heavy heelmarks.

They went back to the bedroom. Somebody was hammering on the hall door, and when Morton opened it McGarvey tumbled in, breathless.

"No sign of young Wetmore anywhere. Nobody remembers seeing him for the past half hour, but several people saw him come upstairs then. Nothing in the maid's room, but here's some stuff we found in young Wetmore's room. See; the handwriting matches that note perfect! And these are some pictures."

He frowned upon the master of the house. "Looks pretty bad for your son. I might as well tell you that right now."

CAPTAIN MONTGOMERY GOT down to headquarters early, and attracted by an odor of rank cigar smoke, looked into the office Detective Morton shared with young Detective McGarvey.

"Geez, don't you ever go to bed?" he asked.

"I been thinking," Morton explained apologetically.

"Don't strain yourself. They pick up that Wetmore kid yet?"

"I been thinking," Morton said, "that it wasn't young Wetmore after all. I explained it to the kid, too, but he says I'm nuts."

"Garv gets things right sometimes."

"When?"

"Don't be too tough on that kid, Mort. He's got to learn, hasn't he? After all, he means well. And he just about worships you."

"That's nice."

"I know you'd rather work alone, but you really ought to have somebody around with you. You got to admit Garv drives a car good."

"Yeah."

"And he's got plenty of guts," the captain added.

"So has a prize bull, probably. But since when have I been putting in requisitions for prize bulls?" Morton demanded.

"Garv's husky too. That might come in handy some-time."

"Yeah, if I should happen to have some railroad ties I wanted busted in half, or a court house I wanted tore down, he'd probably be a lot of help."

"Anyway," said the captain, "I got to agree with him about you being nuts on this thing. It's as plain as anything could be that young Wetmore had an affair with that maid and wrote her some foolish notes, and she was trying to hold him up. He just overlooked one of the notes when he ran out."

"In the middle of a party, when she'd be as busy as him?"

The captain shrugged. "Maybe she threatened to go

downstairs and expose him before all those people, if he didn't disgorge. He got panicky and tried to stab her. She jumped for the phone, and he started to choke her with the first thing he could find."

"What would young Wetmore be doing with a knife? And even supposing he had it, why should he slash her five or six times in the side instead of sticking it right into her? Any damn fool would know that that isn't any way to kill a pretty young blackmailer! And why should he go stamping off on his heels, making deeper prints than even I made? He only weighs"—Morton glanced at the description form from which the general alarm had been sent out—"a hundred and twenty-two. And as I get it, he was practically sober last night, for a change." Morton picked up a large photograph. "Course, I'm no doctor. And we won't get the autopsy for a couple of hours yet. But the way that girl's face looked, I'd be ready to bet she was killed by strangulation and not by any pin pricks in her side. People that're dead already don't bleed much, and there was an awful lot of blood there." He tapped the photograph. "I don't like the position of that body. Something funny about it. It looks to me somehow as if it had been placed that way, and couldn't maybe that mean that somebody wanted it to look as if the cuts in the side were responsible for all the blood?"

"Maybe? But in that case, where did the blood come from?"

"That," Morton explained, "is what I been thinking about."

ONE OTHER ITEM among the papers which littered his desk interested Morton. It was a freshly printed tack-up calling for the arrest of Henry M., "Henny," Pirbright, alias

Pincher, alias Potts, etc., etc. A very bad man, this one. A specialist in violence, and undoubtedly a killer. It never had been possible to make a murder rap stick to him, for four years before he'd been sent to the state prison at Rayford for a life term on a charge of manslaughter. Now he was free, after a sensational break the previous day. He was wanted, dead or alive. Preferably—the tack-up all but said in so many words—dead.

Morton put on his hat and went to see James Corlis, retired sheriff. These two sat in a couple of creaky rocking chairs and chatted of old times. Corlis said it was too bad about McGarvey, senior, and Morton said it sure was—there was one good guy, old McGarvey. Corlis asked what Gary's son was like, now that he was a detective, and Morton said that it was sort of like having a small-ish elephant travel around with you except that you could probably teach an elephant some tricks. Corlis said, well the kid would learn, give him time. Morton said he doubted it.

Then suddenly Morton put his question. Corlis was amazed and hurt.

"What the hell makes you think I'm that kind of a guy?"

"I know. I know. But this is mighty important, Jim. Maybe even a matter of life and death." He leaned closer, and his face was grave. "Listen, Jim. Somebody turned in Pirbright four years ago—that's a cinch! You didn't get any vision from heaven!"

"So what?"

"Well, does Henny himself know who it was?" Morton asked.

"Sure he knows. The guy knew Henny was going to get life or else he wouldn't have dared to squeal. It was fixed."

"Henny," Morton pointed out, "never was spilling over with the milk of human kindness. He wasn't going around turning the other cheek."

"I'd thought about that."

"This guy's still in Miami, maybe? I'm looking for a guy that was in an awful hurry about something last night. And while I don't think that Henny would have the nerve to come back here, still and all—"

"If I could be sure," said Corlis, "that you wouldn't even loosen up to that youngster you got working with you—"

It was Morton's turn to look hurt. He clucked his tongue.

"I'm ashamed of you, Jim."

Corlis, former sheriff, relighted his pipe. He made quite a ceremony of it, and afterward, without looking at Morton, he said: "It was Joey McIntyre."

Then, for some time, they chatted further about the old days, agreeing that it had been better when Miami was a nice quiet place where nice quiet people came to live, and you weren't forever stumbling over drunken millionaires—when the beach was still just a sandbar, and Biscayne Boulevard and Flagler Street were crossable by poor fools afoot—when Coral Gables was the name of a farm, and the Peacock out in Coconut Grove was considered a most acceptable hostelry in spite of the fact that it charged a whole dollar a day American plan—in short, when cops still had time to sit around like this and talk.

"Well, thanks for the dope," Morton said, when finally he rose.

McGARVEY WAS OPENING windows. "Smells like an alligator farm on a hot day. What's new? They tell me outside that there's no word on that Wetmore kid yet."

"We ain't looking for Wetmore now."

"What d'yuh mean, we ain't looking for Wetmore?" The junior partner started to bluster—but he stopped when he saw that Morton was paying him no attention. Whenever he was in doubt, which was much of the time, young McGarvey tried to cover it by acting tough. It impressed some people; but it did not seem to impress this cool, gray, impersonal man. McGarvey, indeed, was not at all sure of what Morton thought of him, and he was worried about this. If Morton didn't like him, didn't like to work with him, McGarvey would be paired off with some other detective. "Well then—who do we look for, huh?"

"A guy named Joey McIntyre. Know him?"

McGarvey simply couldn't understand this. "What the hell has that tin-horn got to do with it?"

"You do know him then?" Morton persisted.

"Sure I know him. Saw him only day before yesterday. They tell me he's broke as hell and can't even manage to borrow anything any more."

"That's fine. Go out and scrape up some more stuff like that. I want to get a shave and some breakfast, and I'll meet you here in two hours."

"Want me to pick up McIntyre, if I find him?"

"No. If he's in sight at all he's not the man we want."

But Joey McIntyre, McGarvey reported later, was not in sight. Nobody had seen him since the previous afternoon. Garv had been to his hotel room, searched the place, found nothing of any significance.

"He's been hanging around the dog tracks, and losing plenty. Don't seem to be working any particular racket, but he's been boasting that he'll have a flock of jack soon. The

only guy he goes around with these days is Louie Washman, but I can't locate Louie either."

"Women?"

"None that he goes around with where anybody sees
him, but occasionally he's been seen driving with a small
brunette, nights."

Morton smiled. "Small brunette, huh? Wouldn't be she'd
look like a maid maybe?"

McGarvey gasped. "Say, I never thought of that!"

"The other servants said Ellen Wilcox had a boy friend
but she wouldn't talk about him and he never came to the
house. Used to park down the street and she'd walk down
and get in. He had a big, old sedan, they said. Well, Joey
drives a five-year-old Cadillac sedan."

"Say, you sure do find out things, don't you!" McGarvey's
eyes were bright with admiration. "Joey McIntyre's the
last person in the world I'd have figured to be mixed up in
anything like this. How'd you ever get that hunch, anyway?"

Morton asked: "You see that runt, Silvers?"

"He wasn't in. Don't come on till two o'clock."

"We'll get him then," Morton decreed. "Sammy Silvers
knows more about the bad boys in this town than they do
themselves."

The autopsy report would have caused almost any cop
but Wentworth L. Morton to break into I-told-you-so's. It
said that death had been caused by strangulation and that
the superficial cuts on the left side apparently had been
inflicted afterward.

There was a wire from Providence, R.I., the late Ellen
Wilcox's home city. The Providence police knew nothing
of her. There were other odds and ends like this, nothing

of importance. There was no further word of the escaped convict, Henry Pirbright. Morton took another long look at Pirbright's likeness on the tack-up, and he smiled mirthlessly. Certainly a tough customer. Thin gritty face, loose mouth, eyes that were narrow and hard. Better shoot first if you should meet up with this Pirbright proposition, Morton reflected.

At two o'clock Morton and McGarvey spread their elbows on the lunch counter where Sammy Silvers did the waiting. Silvers was a tiny, jumpy fellow. He loved Miami, and his greatest fear was that some day the cops, knowing what they did about his past, would chase him out. He had ears as big as the city itself, and could be useful.

"Geez, you guys ain't here on business, are you?"

"Just wanted to ask you a few questions, that's all, Sammy."

Silvers glanced nervously toward the kitchen, then to the left, toward the sidewalk entrance. He rubbed his hands on his apron.

"We figured you wouldn't like it to be here, so we parked the car up the street a little ways, near Flagler. We'll see you there." They started for the door, Sammy Silvers was whispering rapid, passionate protests. "You better come," Morton said gently.

McGarvey took the wheel. Morton sat in back. And presently Silvers came scuttling along like a frightened rabbit. Morton opened a door.

"In here, Sammy. I knew you wouldn't disappoint us."

BY FOUR THIRTY Silvers, his apron on again, was back behind his counter, while Morton and McGarvey stared across a flat expanse of weeds toward a pink stucco house.

They were behind a clump of pines, almost the only cover for half a mile around.

"Lousy lay," McGarvey decided. "We're not even sure they're in there, either. Might be better if we walked up, just casual."

"No good. We both walk cop, no matter how hard we try not to. They couldn't miss us."

Once a realtor had fondly hoped that the city would grow out to this house; but the city, after great dreams exploded, hadn't; so the house stood alone. The sidewalks already had cracked and crumbled, and the street itself, though paved, was losing a long and soundless struggle to the encroaching jungle. The street led nowhere. There were no houses beyond this one, none near it.

"Suppose we just dash up in the car and jump out?"

"Suppose we don't. They'd know the shake of a department Chevvy just like they'd know the gait of a cop. And yet if we call a squad, and it turns out nobody was there, we'd get the merry tee-hee for months. Tell you what. You drive over to the Trail and ask my friend Ben Green for a loan of one of his delivery trucks. Tell him it's for me. He runs a market just below Twenty-sixth. I'll stick around here."

Through a considerable wait, for this was far out, Morton saw no sign of life around the pink stucco house. But this fact did not dishearten him. Silvers had said that the place was well stocked with food, and that Joey McIntyre kept it rented in another name for just such emergencies as this one. Joey could lie low there for a month or more, Silvers had said, and nobody would be any the wiser.

Joey McIntyre spoke of himself as an "operator," by

which he meant that he thought himself a big-time gambler. So he was, too, sometimes. But he had his ups and downs, like most gamblers, and recently the downs had predominated. Joey, once a dandy and very loud of speech, had degenerated to a mere hanger-on, a no-account crook and petty racketeer. He still lolled back in his big old sedan, while his friend, and faithful bodyguard, Louie Washman drove; he still smoked cigars and talked big; but it was generally believed around Miami that his day had come and gone and was unlikely to return.

Still, you never knew. Joey wasn't stupid. Washman might be, but not Joey. And Washman, whatever his mental shortcomings, was no slouch with a pistol. Neither was Joey himself, for that matter. Altogether, Morton didn't like it.

McGarvey was perspiring, and very red of the face, when he jounced into sight.

"A pal, that guy Green! I mention your name, and look what I get! This thing ought to be in the Smithsonian Institute."

Morton climbed in. "Let's hope it gets us to the house," he said.

McGarvey did not diminish speed as they approached the discouraged, undernourished-looking house. But directly in front, he ground the brakes down, and he and Morton piled out and ran to the porch.

On the porch the only article of furniture was a taboret bearing, reluctantly, a lard tin filled with chalky earth in which some poor plant had long since languished and died. Two windows and the front door faced upon this porch.

Morton and McGarvey got close to the wall, on either side of the door, and Morton knocked.

Nothing. Only the echoes.

McGarvey whispered: "You know, I got a hunch they're in there anyway. I just feel that!"

Morton nodded solemnly, and knocked again, very hard.

The whole place was horribly still. It had the air of a house which never had been occupied at all—a dream unfulfilled, a hope gone sour, gathering dust. The pale pink stucco, scorched by the sun, peeled listlessly, leaving grayish blotches upon the walls. In front, weeds fought for possession of a discouraged, almost invisible pathway and a preposterous little garden-gate. Creepers and rank grasses, hedging the building on all sides, seemed to try to blot out its existence.

The detectives tried the front door and found it locked. They walked around the house, trying to peer through window glass encrusted with grime. They had the feeling that somebody was watching them.

The back door was locked. It was flimsier than the front door.

THEY RETURNED TO the front. McGarvey was all for smashing in; but Morton didn't like to move without a search warrant. After all, they didn't know who owned this place, and they had no proof that any criminal was here. Getting down to it, Morton reasoned, they had very little proof of anything at all; and a busting-in party might result in a nasty kick-back. They were acting, really, on a hunch. The law doesn't recognize hunches. Jim Corlis, Morton knew, could not be expected to make public his secret. It was certain that Silvers would not sign his name to any statement or affidavit—would not repeat his evidence, scant enough anyway, before another person.

"Aye tank we go home," Morton decided.

"Personally, I'd take the chance," McGarvey boasted.

"You would. But not when you've been a cop as long as I have."

They started away, clawed at by a twitchy temptation to jerk their chins over their shoulders, for each still felt that somebody was watching his every movement.

THEY HAD ALMOST reached the idiotic little gate when a scream sounded from the house. A scream—then a scuffle of feet, a dull, thunking sound, and silence. McGarvey spun on his heel, raced up to the porch, threw his weight against the front door.

Morton sprang after him, growling something about kids who read too many magazines.

There was a sound like a couple of boards slapped together. Within a few inches of McGarvey's head a spray of powdery splinters appeared, and below that—one long splinter leaned jaggedly, looking foolish.

Morton snatched the taboret and hurled this through the window on the right. He grabbed McGarvey and led him, crouching, underneath the window on the left, over the porch rail, around to the back of the house. "Use the meat on *this!*" He helped, swinging in unison with McGarvey's enormous body. Three pushes did it. The lock snapped and the door whanged back with a crash that sent scared little echoes tumbling madly all through the house.

Morton dodged against a wall, McGarvey ran straight in. Morton saw a large shadow, fired twice. The shadow seemed to wave like a black sheet in a breeze. There were two other explosions: McGarvey was shooting, and small blasts of flame sprang from the shadow. Morton fired again, and the shadow slid to the floor.

After a moment, as his eyes became accustomed to the darkness, Morton saw that this had been Louie Washman—who wasn't going to do any more shooting. Morton cocked his revolver, cleared his throat soundlessly. When he heard a thin grating from ahead he called to his partner: "Scamper around front, Garv, and burn that baby down the second he sticks his head out."

Silence for a moment. McGarvey, bewildered, instinctively obeyed that cool, hard voice. He started to back away.

Then a frightened whine. "Lay off, you guys! You got no right to bust in here!"

Morton cackled: "Better come back and say hello, Joey. Reaching. Otherwise you get every chunk of lead we have, which is plenty."

"You guys got no right—"

"Are you coming?"

Joey McIntyre always had been yellow. They heard him drop his gun. Slowly, shuffling his feet, he crossed the front room, entered the kitchen. His hands were high, his thin, small face glittered with sweat.

There was no need to worry about Washman, who was emphatically dead. They turned McIntyre around, frisked him, marched him into the front room. There, on a cot, was a young man in dirty dinner clothes. His left shoulder had been crudely bandaged with torn-up shirt-tail, and blood was caked a rusty brown upon this; but upon his forehead was a fresher wound. He was motionless, and his eyes were shut.

"So he let out a yawp and you smacked him, huh?" Morton sneered.

McGarvey picked up the gun McIntyre had dropped, went into the kitchen and scooped up Washman's gun.

"We ought to get a doctor for this kid," Morton said. He looked around the room. The floor was covered only by dust, and there were two cots, a couple of straight-back chairs, a table strewn with newspapers, dope sheets, copies of the daily racing form. In one corner, unexpectedly, was a telephone. It was on the floor. Morton picked it up. "This thing ain't connected, by any chance?" It was. Morton got headquarters, asked for Captain Montgomery. The switch-board man wanted to know if he'd heard about the murder.

"What—another one?"

"Just a little while ago. Just got a flash on it. Guy chucked out of a car out near the Gables. Friend of yours too, I think. Little jerky guy—name's Sam something. Works in a chile joint on the boulevard near the end of the causeway."

MORTON'S EYES GREW thoughtful. So somebody else had been asking Sammy Silvers questions. Somebody who had been in too much of a hurry to prod Sammy with only gentle threats.

"Don't know whether he's really dead or not, but he certainly absorbed an awful shellacking if he ain't, from what we hear. Because—"

"I thought I asked for Montgomery," Morton said to the talkative operator.

While he waited for the captain to answer, Morton placed the mouthpiece against his chest and said to McGarvey: "I hope you're not hungry, Sherlock Holmes, because we got another job right away."

"Where do we go from here?"

"We don't go anywhere. We just sit here and wait."

"For who?" McGarvey queried.

"For a guy that just found out the same thing as we did, only faster, and who ought to be ambling in here any time now. As soon—"

Captain Montgomery's voice came: "Uh-huh?"

"Cap? Listen—here's what I wish you'd do. I wish you'd send—"

Somebody in the kitchen doorway quietly but very clearly said: "Hang up easy, copper, and put it down, and then raise 'em."

McGarvey wheeled, gasping. Morton moved only his eyeballs to see a man with a thin, gritty face, loose mouth, eyes that were narrow and hard. This man held a large automatic pistol in each hand.

"Take it easy, copper. No slam-bangs. I got time for all I want to do anyway, and I don't mind doing a little more if it's necessary."

Montgomery, at headquarters, was rasping: "Well, what the hell is it you want me to send, and where the hell should I send it, and what the hell's the matter with you anyway— you don't say anything?"

McGarvey had the good sense to remain motionless. Morton, very quietly, very carefully, hung up; quietly and carefully he replaced the telephone; then he raised his arms. McGarvey, too, had raised his arms. As for Joey McIntyre, he was in some outer region of terror, beyond sanity. He had virtually fainted on his feet; and the only thing about him that moved was the sweat rolling pauselessly down his face and dripping off his chin in cold, pear-shaped drops.

"I been waiting four years for this." Out of a corner of his mouth, without moving his head or eyes, Henry Pirbright called: "Sol!"

It had been known, from the nature of the break, that Pirbright had received outside help. The man who came into the room now was a stranger to Morton, as he was to McGarvey. He was heavy-set, sharp-featured, quick in his movements, no southerner. Dark eyes were utterly cold, face expressionless. In his left hand he held a cocked revolver, but he didn't point this at anybody.

"Turn around, cops."

They turned, faced the wall, and presently a hand went over their persons, removing guns.

"I been waiting four years for this," Pirbright repeated softly. "You guys can turn around and look, if you want. It don't mean a thing to me. As long as you behave yourselves I won't hurt you, much."

THEY TURNED, KEEPING their hands high. McGarvey, usually given to big talk when there was any trouble, now was silent. But the phlegmatic Morton began to talk rapidly.

"The state'll save you the trouble, Pirbright. We're pinching Joey on a murder charge right now, and he'll get everything surer'n hell, because that guy on the cot's going to make a perfect witness."

Pirbright smiled a little. "I don't trust the state. Four years I been promising myself this fun, anyway." He stared somberly at Joey McIntyre. "But when did this louse ever get the guts to croak a guy?"

"It wasn't a guy, it was a girl."

"It would be," Henry scoffed.

"Joey'd been playing around with her on the quiet. She worked for the Wetmores, the folks of this guy on the cot. Rich as hell. Joey wanted to promote a little blackmail, so she giggled a flock of come-on at the old man himself, but it was no soap. Scared his wife'd find out, I suppose. Then she went to work on this kid instead, and he acted up something scandalous. Joey was deep in the soup and he was counting on coming back with some notes this kid had written. But then he heard about you busting Rayford and he decided it'd be best to blow. Only he didn't have any money, and he couldn't borrow any. So he thought he'd better close the deal right away, irregardless. The Wetmores were giving a blowout, but Joey had his punk drive up to a place nearby and he went in the back way, upstairs, and got hold of the girl."

The telephone started to ring. Captain Montgomery had caused the call to be traced, and was trying to get Morton back. But would Montgomery have sense enough to chase out to this place with a squad?

Nobody stirred. The bell made a terrific noise in that dim place. Morton wetted his lips, and the instant the ringing ceased he resumed hastily: "She was probably scared, but she got word down to the kid to meet her in the old man's bedroom, and there they tried to shake him down. All Joey was thinking about was getting some runaway dough. He didn't care how much of a jam he got the dame into."

Pirbright said: "He wouldn't. Not that guy."

"But the kid laughed. What the hell did he care if the girl started a breach of promise action? His old man had plenty. And as for his reputation—hell, that couldn't be any worse, no matter what came out. He's the kind of a kid would be proud of a thing like that anyway, instead of being ashamed. So he tells them to go do things to themselves. Then Joey starts to get panicky and—"

The telephone bell again. Montgomery, sore, had been bawling out the operator, Morton guessed. The bell rang and rang. They all stood listening to it, not moving, and it rang for a long while. When it had stopped the room was filled with bewildered, jumpy little echoes that stung the eardrums.

"So then what?" Henry asked.

"Maybe the kid got tough. I don't know. Anyway, Joey lost his head and pulled a jack knife with a spring handle that I took off him just a few minutes ago, and he gives it to the kid in the shoulder. Meaning to get the neck. The kid goes down, probably fainting from shock and pain, and bleeding like a pig. He looks deader'n hell.

"Then the girl lost *her* head. A little blackmail was one thing, but killings were out. She snatches up the telephone, hysterical, and starts to yell for headquarters. Before she gets put through Joey grabs her around the throat. He grabs a scarf that happens to be handy, and he garrots her. He hangs up the phone, and then he runs outside and slashes the wire where he'd seen it come into the house. He knows that otherwise the operator might start ringing back and somebody downstairs might answer—because this is only an extension. He's hoping that the operator never even heard the girl yell, but he can't count on that.

"He comes back inside and finds the girl dead, but not the kid. The kid's moving maybe, or maybe groaning. So Joey—"

"This is all very interesting," said Pirbright, and waggled

one of his pistols, "But I think we better cut it short. Your boy friends might be coming out for a look pretty soon, and I got a job to do here."

"I want to tell you what a clear case we got against him!" Morton said.

"That wouldn't make any difference to me. I got my own case."

MORTON HURRIED ON. "Joey realizes the kid isn't dead, by an inch or more, and that when he comes to, he'll be able to identify him. He knows he can get out of the place without being seen, and he figures why not take the kid along with him? Why not make a snatch out of it, and at the same time put away the only murder witness? He's always thinking of getting dough, because he's got to have it to breeze, and he figures he'd better breeze a long, long ways to be safe."

"Then he figured wrong. I'd have followed the mug to China!" Pirbright cut in.

"He starts to pick up the kid, who doesn't weigh much, but then he sees all that blood and he gets what he thinks is a bright idea. He throws the girl's body down there and slashes her a bit above where the blood is, thinking that'll fool somebody, but being too dumb to know that people don't bleed after they're dead like an autopsy will show. Then he picks the kid up, and walks out with him the same way he came in, and joins Washman, who's waiting, and they come out here."

McGarvey was gaping at him like a boy watching a sleight-of-hand artist extracting bowls of goldfish from his coat pockets. But Pirbright shook an impatient head.

"That's mighty bright, copper, and I appreciate your telling me about it, but I got something else to do right now."

Pirbright started to walk toward Joey McIntyre. He was holding both guns rather high.

"If you guys want to watch this, it's O.K. by me. Only if you don't like things like this, you better turn the other way right about now."

It was horrible to watch that slow walk across the room—that deliberate, cold-blooded walk, that cold-blooded smile on Pirbright's mouth. McIntyre himself seemed past all emotion, even fear. He gave a little wheezy sigh, and, still with his eyes wide open, slid to the floor in a swoon. Henny Pirbright grabbed him gently, almost lovingly, and yanked him up to a kneeling position. He placed one of the pistols squarely against McIntyre's face.

McGarvey yelled: "Hey, you can't do that!" and sprang at Pirbright.

Sol took a step forward from the kitchen door, firing. McGarvey staggered, half-turned, but plunged straight on for Henny Pirbright. Pirbright was shooting his whole gun out into McIntyre's mouth. McGarvey punched him in the left ear and they both crashed to the floor.

It made Morton a little sick. He howled something meaningless, and dived at Sol's legs.

Even in that instant, even through the thunder of guns, Morton heard the siren's wail. And even in that instant he cursed all cops who worked sirens just for show-off purposes, while driving through streets where there was no traffic and where there were no blind corners.

Yet it was the siren which saved his life. He got his arms around Sol's knees and hugged them tight, pulling his own legs up underneath him. He felt rather than heard an explosion against the top of his head, and he felt a burn of pain there. His ears thumped and his eyes felt flame-seared.

They went down, Sol twisting so that Morton was underneath. Then, inexplicably, Sol wasn't there. He was running out through the kitchen, leaving Morton on the floor.

For Sol too had heard that siren.

Morton got to his knees, got to his feet.

Henry M., "Henny", Pirbright, alias Pincher, alias Potts, etc., etc., had a gun in each hand still, but a semi-conscious McGarvey clung insanely to the right wrist, while the left was in the grip of a wholly unconscious, and, in fact hideously dead, Joey McIntyre. McIntyre must have made one last convulsive grasp at that wrist.

Pirbright swerved, pulling away, cursing wildly. McGarvey's grip broke, and the big detective fell flat upon his face; but the lifeless fingers of what had been little Joey McIntyre were fingers of steel. Morton, bellowing, hit Pirbright full in the chest with both hands at once, and knocked him over backward. Morton fell upon him, madly battered his head against the floor. Then, when Pirbright was still, Morton sat upon him.

THAT WAS THE position in which Captain Montgomery and the others found him a few moments later—sitting on top of what seemed to be a tangle of corpses, moaning, holding his head between his hands.

They lifted him, walked him around the room. He wasn't badly hurt, only stunned. After a time he shook his head, wiped his face, pushed them away without comment.

Captain Montgomery said: "Henny Pirbright, eh? I

thought you two were supposed to be working on that Wetmore case?"

"They got mixed up somehow," Morton muttered.

He rode back in the ambulance with McGarvey. He was all right now, not even dizzy any longer, though his head ached. Garv had a broken shoulder and he'd lost a lot of blood, but he was conscious.

"That was a break, that guy Pirbright busting in like that," McGarvey cried. "What do you suppose he was sore at Joey about?"

"I wouldn't know." Morton put his elbows on his knees and held his head between his hands, rocking a little. "The only thing I wish is that they'd have a little consideration for a guy's head and stop working that damn siren out there."

McGarvey cleared his throat nervously. "Mort—I don't know, maybe this is a bad time to ask you—"

"What's the matter with you now?" Mort groaned.

"I just thought—I mean, don't you think we get along all right? Don't you think maybe we'd make a couple of good sidekicks, like you and my old man used to be—maybe?"

"Your old man had brains."

"Yeah, I know. I know I'm dumb. But I thought maybe—"

"Sure, you're all right, kid. Don't mind me. I always get crabby when bullets have been creasing my knob like this. Sure, I guess we ought to get along all right. You'll be swell to have around in case we run out of gas and I need somebody to carry the car on his back."

"You mean that? I mean, no kidding?"

"Sure."

"Geez, that'll be swell," said young McGarvey.

MURDER BY PROXY

Heart Island was a little corner of Paradise until murder landed there and changed it overnight to a horror haven. But Morton and McGarvey, that amazing team of coppers, were change artists after their own fashion and it didn't take them long to shift things back to their original state with a little lead directed at the right targets.

1

DIAMONDS ARE TRUMPS

THE MEN STOPPED in the shadow of a big hibiscus bush
to fasten black silk masks across their faces, and to draw
their weapons. The taller man had two automatic pistols.
The other had a Thompson sub-machine gun.

They moved boldly across the lawn toward the mansion
where Harrison Rawlins was entertaining his neighbors
at bridge. Rawlins was called the Mayor of Heart Island,
which was not really an island at all since the lower end
of it was connected with the mainland by a thirty-foot
causeway. Once it had been no more than mud flats, but
Rawlins and his money had converted it into a celebrated
paradise; he had landscaped it, built the canal and yacht
basin and constructed the causeway. He had apportioned
the whole into six equal parts, sold five of these parts to
five of his friends, and himself occupied one of the finest
sites—his buff-stucco, Mediterranean-style house had the
canal on one side. On the other side and in front were the
waters of Biscayne Bay. Now, people visited Heart Island
as they might visit a museum, and talked with up-caught
breath about the men who lived there—especially about
Harrison Rawlins.

This night was very quiet, and warm. There was almost

*Morton held his pistol
in his teeth and jumped*

no breeze to rustle the coconut palms. A low, full moon, quite as lavish as Rawlins himself but much more democratic, smeared its light over houses, garages, gardens and lawns. Over white, unrocking cruisers in the yacht basin, and most gloriously over the smooth surface of the bay.

"You take the windows," the taller man whispered. "I'm taking the door."

It was only half past nine, and the card-playing had just begun. There were two tables, four men and four women.

When the bandits entered, all four of the men sprang to their feet, raising their arms. Rawlins, himself, was a big fellow in the prime of life, well proportioned, good-looking, a famous halfback in his college days. He had the self-assurance of one who had found it easy to beat men or to make money, easier still to acquire women. Carpenter was tall, thin, dark. An aristocrat gone bad, he controlled the remnants of a fortune once great. Potter was little and tubby, with grayish hair, dreamy blue-gray eyes, an absent-minded smile. Campbell was a middle-aged business man, retired, the only year-round resident of the island.

"Back against the wall, you guys!"

A woman fainted spectacularly.

Another rose, tried to scream, started to run toward the back of the house, and fell with a crash to her knees. The rest of the women didn't stir. They simply didn't get a chance to be frightened.

The tall man pocketed his automatics. He moved quickly toward Mrs. Rawlins, a thin, pretty woman. Without unnecessary violence, but firmly, he jerked away her necklace, started to fumble for her rings.

The shorter man yelled: "Look out! He's grabbin' fer something!" and started to shoot.

Harrison Rawlins, big though he was, thumped back against the wall. His body jerked four or five times, pushing backwards, as though he were trying to dig into the wall with his shoulder blades. His eyes were wide open, and his mouth was open too. He seemed not terrified, only astounded. When the shooting stopped, he turned right a little, then a little left. He swung forward away from the wall and abruptly, eager blotches of blood appeared in half a dozen places on his shirt front. Gradually he toppled full-length, face down, across one of the bridge tables.

The butler dropped a tray. One of the women, thrown on her back by Rawlins' fall, screamed shrilly. Another woman ran crazily for the green baize door, screaming even more piercingly. The gunmen disappeared as suddenly as they had come.

Harrison Rawlins was emphatically dead, and play-ing-cards were strewn over the floor. Carpenter jumped for the telephone.

"Police headquarters, operator! Give me police head-quarters!"

McGARVEY BEING YOUNG and healthy, and in love with his job, usually drove fast even when he wasn't responding to an emergency call. This night, he reached the wheel of the speedy cruiser before the desk sergeant had hung up the receiver, and he was starting the car when Morton, older, much more sedate, clambered in beside him. McGarvey drove as fast as the car would go.

"That'd be Patrol Eighteen," he yelled. "Who's on that, Mort?"

"Never mind who's on it. Flaherty and young McIn-tyre, if you must know. But Geez, kid, watch where you're driving!"

Morton had known lots of excitement. Too much of it. He preferred things quiet. What he was chiefly thinking about—aside from the fact that they'd probably both get killed, the way McGarvey was driving—was the chance that poor old Church might have been hurt. Church was employed by the six owners of Heart Island, and lived in a little stone gatehouse; but when Morton had known him best, Church was an active cop and a mighty good pinochle player. He and Morton and McGarvey's father had sat up at pinochle many a long, slow night. That game had been an institution in the Miami city police department, and other cops swore that it was immortal, that it would go on forever and ever. But it hadn't. Church had been forced to retire because of poor health and later, unable to get back

on the force, he had got the watchman job. Soon afterward, young McGarvey's father, as grand an old-time cop
as ever anybody met, had been shot through the heart by
a snowed-up gangster from Detroit.

"Ain't they got some kind of watchman or something
out there?"

"Do you have to make the turns like that, Garv? Yes, old
Joe Church works there."

"We ought to make it only a few minutes after the
radio patrol. Joe Church—wasn't he one of my old man's
buddies?"

"He was," grunted Morton, and gave up trying to light
a cigar. There wasn't much to do but hold on.

"Maybe we can catch whoever it was coming out. There's
only one way they can get out. Here we are!"

The car swung on two wheels into the causeway, started
for the gate next to Church's little stone house.

Something dark emerged from that gate. McGarvey
yelled, twisted the wheel. The cruiser wasn't quite straight
when the metal clashed, the rubber shrieked. Sighing noisily, tired, grateful for the chance to rest, it slid over upon
its right side.

Morton had moved fast, had jumped. He landed upon
his hands and knees among the jagged pieces of coral
which lined the causeway. It cut badly but he paid no heed
to this. He was up instantly, and scrambling for McGarvey.

"I'm all right! Never mind me! Get that guy that hit us!"

Morton ran back to the road, yanking out his pistol. The
dark car, a small sedan, had kept its balance. It was speeding
south, a diminishing blot in the moonlight. Morton fired
five shots after it. He didn't really expect to hit a tire—he

hoped only to scare the driver into stopping. But the sedan sped on, out of sight.

Morton was fussing around McGarvey with hen-like solicitude, when a uniformed cop, young McIntyre, one of the two on the radio patrol that night, ran through the gateway.

"That you, Mort? You see a car come out of here just now?"

"Never mind that. It's gone for good, now. Help me get Barney Oldfield here, out of this junk heap."

McGarvey cried: "I'm all right. It's just that I got a couple of slices from that glass, and for a second there that wheel gave me such a poke that it was like getting smacked in the solar plexus when you didn't expect it. But I'm all right."

"Flaherty's inside! Somebody's got killed, I hear! I ran back when I saw that car start out," McIntyre broke in.

Morton rumbled: "It's a wonder, with all them fancy radios and things you guys got—it's a wonder you couldn't sometimes—"

"The guy must've been underneath a big mangrove in there, where you couldn't see him at first. He didn't have his lights on. We didn't see him till we flashed past, almost in front of Rawlins' house, and by that time he'd started up the other way—started for out here."

They found Joe Church just inside the door of the gate-house, which was unlocked. The back of the watchman's head was bloody, and he was unconscious. But his telephone still was working.

"... a Ford sedan, or maybe a Rambler. Small, anyway. Dark blue color. Some of the paint got scraped off. The left running board and the left back fender'd be pretty badly dented, I should think, and maybe the front fender on that side. Probably the hub caps, too. Call 'em down as far as Florida City and Homestead and Matecumbe. And if you get any word at all, give me a ring at Harrison Rawlins' house. Now listen. Send an ambulance up here for Joe Church… What?… Yeah, somebody slapped a concussion on him, and he's out like a light."

To McIntyre, when he'd hung up, Morton snarled: "Stick around here, Sherlock, and don't let anybody out—and don't let anybody in, either, that ain't got any business there, see?"

Then, a little late, and on foot, he and McGarvey went to the home of the late Harrison Rawlins.

MORTON, WHEN THE first flush of excitement had ebbed, looked just tired. In appearance, there was nothing of the sleuth, the man-hunter, about Morton. He was no Sherlock Holmes. He was a cop, and didn't pretend to be anything else. But he was a good cop. Moreover, he was a good friend—if he was your friend at all.

His feet dragged a bit as he returned from the hospital. He had big, deliberate feet; and though he was a man of no more than ordinary build—he looked almost little by the side of McGarvey—he always had moved heavily, slowly.

He found McGarvey shuffling reports, photographs, memos. "Got nothing new. But those guys'll show up yet, somewhere! They got to! There was almost enough paint scraped off that can to put on another car, and we got a general alarm out all over the state!"

Morton sat down. He did not remove his hat. He picked up an autopsy report and learned what he already knew—that Harrison Rawlins had been killed instantly. Three slugs had been taken out of the body. Three more had been taken out of the wall, having passed completely through Rawlins.

"The Sweeney men were here. I told them we'd be interested to see anything they turned up but that we were working on the thing from an angle of our own. I don't want them to go and grab all the publicity when we do get these guys cornered! One of them said he heard Rawlins was a great ladies' man, but I don't see what that—" Garv left his question unfinished.

Even McGarvey, babbling youngster though he was, and still thrilled to find himself a detective, sensed that there was something wrong with his companion. Morton never was talkative. But now Morton seemed to have descended to a deeper silence. McGarvey looked sharply at him. Morton had put aside the autopsy report and was making little, meaningless remarks on the back of a "wanted" poster.

"Any chance of Church coming to and giving us some dope? You just come from there, didn't you?"

"Yeah."

"How is he?"

"He's dead," Morton said, and went on making little marks.

McGarvey, who could be almost sensible sometimes, only nodded. He pretended to go on working.

After a time, Morton stopped making the little marks.

"Look, Garv. That makes me kind of sore. Joe Church getting socked like that."

"Sure," said McGarvey. "It was a lousy trick. But we'll

get the lugs! Couple of street-corner sports, probably, too damn lazy to work and out trying to imitate Jesse James."

Morton said quietly: "That wasn't any small-time job, Garv. It wasn't even a stick-up, really. It was a murder."

"Sure it was a murder. It was two murders."

"That isn't what I mean. I mean it was figured for a murder in the first place."

2

HABITANTS OF HEART ISLAND

McGARVEY LEANED BACK, getting excited again. Morton was drawing a rough diagram of Heart Island.

"No jellybeans are going to go pulling a job like that, kid, and you know it. In the first place, there was bound to be a big stink made about it. Rawlins had pull enough to keep us running our cans off for weeks, and the Sweeney Agency had the place protected—Joe Church worked for them really, you know. And then there was the insurance companies that had the jewelry insured. Whoever started on that job knew damn well he was poking up a hornet's nest. Would any street-corner cowboys do that just on the chance of grabbing some ice that would be hot as hell? Suppose they'd cleaned the place out, how much would they have got? Not more'n a thousand or fifteen hundred dollars worth of stuff they'd have one hell of a hard time getting rid of, wouldn't they? They'd be lucky if they fenced one-sixth of that for it. It wasn't as though this was some formal function. It was nothing but a bunch of neighbors in to play cards.

"Now look. Two guys pulled this job, and maybe there was a third guy in the car—if that car had anything to do with it really, which I personally don't believe it did. One guy had a couple of automatics and the other guy had a machine gun. Machine guns aren't so easy to get, Garv my boy, and they aren't so cheap either!"

"Well, these might have been a mob of Northerners that—"

"Now wait. These guys, whoever they were, tapped Joe Church from the back and crushed his skull in. And what's more, they knew they'd done that, too! They didn't try to just put him to sleep. They were after killing him. Otherwise they'd have taken his gun from him, and pulled out the telephone wires in his little house there, or else they'd have tied him up or taped him, wouldn't they? These guys were killers! That was what they set out to do—kill! We got to go over there pretty soon and talk to everybody again, now that things have quieted down a bit, but from what we could get from them last night nobody saw Harrison Rawlins reach for a gun or make any move whatever. The man with the typewriter just yelled something, and then he turned it on. Did he shoot at anybody else? No. All he did was send six hot slugs through Harrison Rawlins and then they both blew. You notice they seemed to have the place pretty well boxed, too? They knew where they were going when they came in, one through the door and one through those big windows."

"You mean you think it was an inside job? We had those servants here for four hours last night, and the widow says—" McGarvey broke in.

"I didn't say I thought it was the servants, did I? You didn't know old Joe Church like I did, Garv. Joe wasn't as young as he used to be, maybe, but there wasn't a thing wrong with his hearing. And he wasn't the kind of cop to go falling asleep and letting people sneak up behind him. But if he knew the guy that came up, that would be different."

"I think you're crazy," McGarvey said.

"Maybe. But wouldn't anybody who knew how things were—supposing they were as goofy as to want to stick up a place like that for practically nothing—wouldn't they know that they were likely to get trapped on that causeway? Matter of fact, Flaherty and young McIntyre weren't more than a quarter of a mile off when they got the flash, and they were there in no time at all. Do you think smart guys would pull a job like that when they'd know they might have to shoot their way out? That don't make sense to me, Garv. If it was for a big stake you might expect somebody to take a wild chance like that maybe, but it wasn't," Morton reasoned.

"That automobile was underneath a mangrove tree, right on the road almost in front of Rawlins' house. And Flaherty and McIntyre said it started away just as they flashed past it," retorted McGarvey.

"That still doesn't prove the automobile was used in the job, does it? I got a strong hunch it wasn't," sighed Morton.

"What are you trying to get at, anyway?"

"I got an idea," Morton said, "that the whole thing was an inside job of some kind, and that the killers never intended to make a break off the island at all."

"But if they never made a break, then they'd be there yet!"

"I got an idea," said Morton, rising, "that that's just where they are. Let's go back and ask some more questions."

HEART ISLAND WAS crowded, not with curious citi-

zens, who were not being admitted—for the whole island
was private property—but with insurance investigators,
uniformed policemen, city detectives in plain clothes, and
representatives of the Sweeney Agency.

The canal, about thirty feet broad, extending the half-
mile from the bay to the yacht basin, cut the island almost
in half. Three houses were on one side of the canal, three
on the other. Between the basin and the causeway were
formal gardens.

The furthest houses from the gateway were, on the right
Rawlins', on the left, Hart Potter's. The canal itself was not
occupied, except by a long, sleek speedboat moored in front
of the Potter house.

"We'll go to the ex-marks-the-spot first," Morton
decided.

The Rawlins house, oddly, seemed deserted. Morton,
followed by McGarvey, pushed into the drawing room—
then stopped, both saying, "Oh."

Ernest Carpenter, his aristocratic features always dark,
but now darker than usual, broke the embrace swiftly and
stepped back.

"Must you come stamping in like this? Isn't Mrs. Rawlins
ever to get a moment's peace?"

"I'm sure sorry," Morton murmured. "Guess I should
have rung."

"Well, I should think so! You policemen let the murderers run away right in front of your noses, and then, when
it's too late to do anything about it, you come barging into
private homes without any warning while I was—uh—I
was offering Mrs. Rawlins my condolences."

"I'm sorry," Morton repeated. "We're going all around

to every house, asking the people if they can't remember anything more than they told us last night. Is it true, Mrs. Rawlins, that you and your husband weren't getting along well?"

"Certainly not! I don't know where you ever heard such a story!"

Carpenter snapped: "Utter nonsense! I think it's an outrage, asking Mrs. Rawlins such a question at a time like this!"

Morton shrugged. Argument would gain him nothing, he knew. These people had money and influence, and the widow, just now, had public sympathy. They could make a lot of trouble for a poor detective.

"You're a bachelor, aren't you, Mr. Carpenter?"

"I am. But I don't see what that has to do with it. Wouldn't it be better if you devoted yourself to catching the robbers instead of asking questions which are an insult to Mrs. Rawlins and to me?"

"Just checking up," Morton explained. "You live in that yellow house across the canal?"

"That's correct. With my sister, Miss Adele Carpenter."

"Does either of you know whether Mr. Rawlins had any enemies?"

The widow started. "Why, no. Harrison always was—" She looked at Carpenter, who was looking at her. "He did have a little run-in with Mr. Spofford the other day, coming to think of it."

"That's the man who's got the second house down?"

"Yes. Harrison resented the fact that he'd been able to lease the place. Harrison always took such pride in Heart Island."

"And what'd he have against this guy Spofford?" Morton queried.

Carpenter volunteered: "Mr. Rawlins knew Spofford in Wall Street, and he knew the man didn't have a very good reputation there. I hate to say this about anybody, but it's pretty much an open secret. And besides that he's not— well, he's not exactly the kind of person we wished to have here on Heart Island."

"They have a fight, then?"

Carpenter looked at the widow. She continued the explanation. "Only the day before yesterday, when Harrison and I were strolling down to where the yachts are, this man Spofford came up to Harrison and accused him of being high-hat, as he expressed it. He was very angry. I think he was a little drunk."

"What did Mr. Rawlins say to that?"

"He told him to keep away from his betters and he wouldn't have anything to worry about. Then this Spofford man got furious. I really think they would have come to blows, if I hadn't been there."

"Did Spofford threaten him, or anything?"

"He didn't threaten to kill him, if that's what you mean. But he did say something like, 'You'd better watch out, that's all.' He called Harrison a dirty stuck-up snob, and a lot of other hard names."

The Rawlins' guest, a Mrs. Alston, was not to be seen. She was in bed, recovering from the shock of the previous evening.

"We'll go and call on Mr. Spofford," Morton decided.

Outside, McGarvey asked eagerly: "Was he really

giving that woman condolences? I couldn't see. I was a little behind you there."

"If those were condolences," Morton grunted, "I hope nobody ever gives my wife any—except me."

"These society people are a lot of bums. I've always said so. And I don't like the looks of that guy Carpenter. They say he's plenty in the red, and how do we know he wasn't fixing to marry this widow?"

"We don't know," Morton admitted, "and what's more, it'd be mighty hard to find out. We got to go easy in this thing."

"Even if Rawlins cut her off, her dower rights would amount to a couple of millions, from all I hear."

THE HOUSE NEXT to Rawlins was unoccupied, the owner being in New York. The grounds had been thoroughly searched, and in the course of a long-distance telephone call, permission had been obtained to search the house itself. Nothing had been found.

Anthony Spofford was a thin man with enormous eyebrows. He had a mean mouth, mean, hard eyes.

"I told you already all I know. I was sitting here on the veranda about half past nine, when all of a sudden I heard the shooting. I didn't even know it was shooting, at the time. Then I heard people yelling, and a little while later a radio car came tearing past hell-bent-for-election, and right after that another car, without any lights, went dashing out. I hadn't seen the other car, before that. It must have been parked underneath that tree up near Rawlins' house. It's pretty dark there, even when the moon's out."

"We're just checking up," Morton apologized.

"Well, that's all I know. There's only me and my wife

here, and three servants. The cook's fat and about fifty. She was up in her room. My chauffeur had the night off, and he was at the pictures. The butler I can answer for because he was right on the veranda with us, serving a drink, when it happened," Spofford offered further.

Spofford lighted a cigar, and the jumping flame made jerky little shadows appear and reappear under his jutting eyebrows. He blew out the match, looked sideways at the two detectives.

"Only one thing, I just happened to think of. None of my damn business, but if it furthers the ends of justice—"

He exhaled, glanced around, waved the cigar. "Campbell over there, lives in that middle house the other side of the canal. He's got an awful good-looking wife, that man."

"Well?"

"Well, Rawlins seemed to think so too. I'm not accusing anybody of anything, you understand! Besides, I don't really know anything—except that I saw 'em walking near here the other night and if they weren't nuts about each other then I'm a woodpecker."

Morton nodded, studying Spofford. He was wondering how best to approach the subject he had come to discuss with this man. He didn't like Spofford's looks. No modern, jaded Wall Street operator, this man, but one of the old school, a pirate with unpatched eye, a buccaneer, the sort of financier who would have been more at home among the Dan Drews and Jay Goulds and Commodore Vanderbilts than among the Owen D. Youngs, Albert Wigginses and Harrison Rawlinses of today.

McGarvey, impatient, exploded the bombshell prematurely. McGarvey was like that. He meant well, but he got excited too easily.

"Listen," he said, shoving forward, "isn't it true that you and Rawlins were on bad terms?"

Spofford looked up sharply, put his cigar into an ashtray. "Sure we were! What of it?"

"Did you have a scrap the other day, right out front here?"

Spofford's face was very dark. His eyes glowed warningly. "I met him out here with his wife, who's always running around with that decayed punk, Carpenter, if that's what you mean. And I asked him why he didn't sometimes act like the gentleman he pretended to be. Sure! He was sore because I managed to rent this place for the season. Thinks I'm not worthy to be mixing with him and his friends. The dirty hypocrite!" Spofford had risen, was waving his arms. "Did he think my money isn't every bit as good as his? The dirty, lousy—"

McGarvey, a little frightened by what he had brought about, stepped forward with outstretched right arm. McGarvey meant to be conciliatory, quieting. Spofford didn't take it that way.

"Keep your damn hands off me!" Spofford shouted.

He shoved McGarvey, who instinctively doubled his huge fists. "Say—" McGarvey moved forward, aggressive now.

Spofford sprang for a table, started to open a drawer. Morton yelled a warning. McGarvey grabbed the banker by an elbow, swung him furiously, sent him reeling across the room, and Spofford fell backward over a chair.

Morton rose, sighing, clucking his tongue. He went to the table, looked into the half-open drawer.

"Sure I got a gun there!" Spofford called. "I got a perfect right to have one in my house!"

"Yeah. But you're not supposed to pull it on cops." Morton closed the drawer, shook his head. "You ought to learn to control that temper of yours, Mr. Spofford."

"We take this guy in, Mort?" Garv asked.

"No. We'll leave him here, and go see Carpenter's sister."

But from the doorway Morton said solemnly: "Only thing is, Mr. Spofford, I wouldn't make a citizen's complaint, if I was you. We don't want to get nasty about this, but we will if we have to."

3

JORGENSEN

McGARVEY, ON THE way across the plaza, was angry. "What's the idea of not picking that bum up? Didn't he go for a gun? Ain't that enough excuse to take him down to headquarters and really ask him something hard?"

"Sure it is, but we wouldn't get anything out of him. Not now. Not the way he's feeling."

"A man with a temper like that's likely to do anything. And what do y' think of what he said about Rawlins and Mrs. Campbell? Say, it's terrible the way these society people act!"

"We'll ask Carpenter's sister about that," Morton said. "But you better let me do the talking this time, Garv, my boy."

She was not very informative. Nervous, still frightened, she remembered very little about the hold-up. And when, very cautiously, Morton approached the subject of Rawlins and Mrs. Campbell, she froze.

"I have heard some talk, but I'm sure it was nothing but malicious gossip. I can't see what business it is of the police, anyway!"

Mrs. Campbell, like Mrs. Rawlins' cousin, was in bed recovering from the shock, and they did not see her. Her husband, trim and cool in doeskins, repeated his story of the hold-up and shooting. He said he had nothing further to add. Carpenter and Mrs. Rawlins? He would rather not talk about that. When Morton persisted, Campbell became chilly.

"I can't understand this. It's the business of the police to catch the thieves, not to go stirring up gossip."

"Sure," said Morton. "Well, you see we're just checking up."

Outside, Morton said playfully: "Getting like regular society guys, ain't we, Garv? Going around calling on millionaires."

"Lot of guinea pigs, if you ask me," McGarvey grumbled. "This was a better place before all these rich people came down here anyway."

Hart Potter was genial, and very helpful when they could get him to stop talking about his flowers.

"Did you ever see tiger lilies like those before? And look at these begonias I've got over here— What's that?... Yes, I live here alone. I'm a married man, but my wife likes to spend her winters in New York."

He employed four servants, but all of them, he said, had been off the previous night. Only one, his valet, lived on the premises.

"We talked to them a while ago," Morton said. "What we wanted to talk to you about now was something a little different."

"Certainly. Anything I can do to help you, I'm glad to. One good rain, at this time of year, and those yuccas over there—"

"That your speedboat in the canal there, Mr. Potter?"

The little fellow straightened, brushing soil from his hands. "I must remember to put that back in the basin. Just plain laziness, leaving it there. Somebody's likely to scrape it, taking one of the cruisers past. Yes, that's mine. You might call that my other hobby, I suppose. Some people like comfortable boats, nice and slow, with big squoshy seats and all that—but me, I like to go fast."

"You drive a car too?" Morton persisted.

"Oh, yes. But I didn't have mine at the Rawlins' last night, if that's what you mean. None of us did. I suppose the others figured the way I did—that it would be nice to walk back. It's longer for me than for the Campbells or the Carpenters, of course, but I don't mind."

The Rawlins house was not far distant, but the canal intervened. Morton nodded toward it.

"Don't suppose there's any way over that canal?"

"Oh, no. You've got to walk all the way around."

Morton dropped his voice, and stared absently at the palm fronds above him. He began asking personal questions.

THE FLOWER ENTHUSIAST wasn't reticent. Yes, he knew about Mrs. Rawlins and Ernest Carpenter. Rawlins and his wife had been getting along badly for years, but he wouldn't give her a divorce because he knew she'd marry Carpenter the moment she was free and he was damned if he'd endow a youngster who never did a day's work in his life.

"There's really no secret about that. Everybody knows it."

Spofford? Why, Spofford was all right, but some of the other residents thought he lowered the tone of the place, and Rawlins in particular was furious when he learned that Spofford had leased a Heart Island house. Rawlins still considered the island his own.

Yes, Potter had heard of the run-in between Rawlins and Spofford. A mean disposition, Spofford had.

As to Rawlins and Mrs. Campbell, he didn't know how serious that had been. Campbell must have heard the whispers. But there was nothing certain. Rawlins had been cautious, fearing to give his wife grounds for divorce.

"You been a lot of help," Morton said, as they prepared to go.

"Not at all! Glad to do my bit, if only for selfish reasons. All these detectives and so forth hanging around, I'm scared that they'll be tramping my flowers. Must they be here, by the way?"

"For a little while, I guess. Just to clear things up. I'll let you know when we call 'em off, which will be as soon as possible."

"Thanks so much. When you go out, gentlemen, I want you to take a look at that bougainvillea over the front verandah."

Driving back to headquarters, McGarvey asked: "So what?"

"I don't know," said Morton, "but I still got an idea my first hunch about the thing was right."

"Meaning you still think the killers are on that island?"

"I still think so, yeah."

"You're a stubborn guy, Mort."

In front of headquarters they found policemen, armed with riot guns and teargas bombs, piling into several cars. One of the Sweeney men had located the small dark sedan with the scraped fenders, and the driver was besieged in a house out in Coconut Grove.

McGarvey swung the little cruiser around on a dime.

"A couple of minutes won't make any difference, now," Morton yelled anxiously, but McGarvey didn't hear him.

They were going sixty-three when they swung into South Miami Avenue and started toward Bayshore Drive.

"Boy-oh-boy!" cried Morton.

THE HOUSE WAS a tiny square one, near the city line of Coral Gables. It stood alone in the middle of a field of weeds. It was singularly quiet, looked deserted. An old Ford sedan stood in back.

Morton asked Captain Montgomery, who was bawling commands: "Regiment in there?"

"No cracks! As far as we know it's only one man, but we ain't taking any chances. It's a crook, anyway. You know him. That Swede, Jorgensen, that just got out of jail about a week ago. One of the Sweeney operatives found the car there and examined it, it's the one, all right. But he didn't want to make the pinch alone, so he was just starting for that big house over by LeJeune Road when he saw Jorgensen run out of here and try to start the car. He yelled and ran towards him, pulling out his gun. Jorgensen yanked out a gun and shot at him twice, and then ran back inside the house. He couldn't get the car started, I guess." Captain Montgomery was visibly excited.

"Sounds more like he lost his head. Jorgensen might have been a burglar, and he might be yet for all I know, but he's no gunman," Mort said.

"He's got a gat," Montgomery went on, "and I don't want to lose anybody. Trouble is, this wall's too far away to throw a tear-gas bomb, and I'm afraid Jorgensen'll start shooting again if we make a rush."

"Probably would, if he's that crazy. Did he hit the Sweeney sleuth?"

"In the right ankle. Busted a bone, I understand."

"Shame," said Morton. He vaulted the wall. "Jorgensen's not a bad fella, if you just talk to him quiet. Tell the boys not to go bang-bang, will you?"

There was a babble of sound behind him, and Montgomery called: "Come back here, you damn fool! You want to get killed?" Morton walked toward the house. He held his hands above his head.

Then there was a voice by his side, and young McGarvey was walking with him.

"I don't know what this is all about," McGarvey growled, "but if you must commit suicide I suppose I ought to be with you."

"Just keep the mitts up," Morton cautioned, "and go slow."

Mostly there were just weeds around them—hot, parched weeds, badly tangled, the color of hay cut too late. There were a few small flower beds lining the path, periwinkles and some gawky, startled poinsettias, but the weeds were choking these.

"If the army back there don't try to rescue us," said Morton, "we ought to be all right."

A voice came from the house: "Stand right where you are!"

They stood. They could see nobody in the house.

Morton called: "Just came to find out what it's all about, Jorg. You know me, don't you?"

"Sure I know you, but I don't know your boy friend."
The voice growled.

"This's young McGarvey. You remember Hash McGarvey? Well, this's his son. Listen. How 'bout me getting closer. I'll wear my lungs out yelling at you from here."

"All right. But your friend can stay where he is."

Morton moved close to the house, stood just outside the front door. He walked slowly, and kept his hands high. But his manner was easy, his voice low and friendly. He could see Jorgensen now. The burglar was in a window at his right, and gripped a revolver.

"Tell papa, Jorg."

"How should I know? A cop I never saw before was snooping around my car back here, and then he starts away, and when I go outside to get in the car he comes running back, pulling a gun on me."

"He's a private dick," Morton explained.

"Well, what's he hanging around my place for?"

"The car, Jorg. You know, the Heart Island job."

"I never had anything to do with that!"

"Did I say you did? But your car was there when it happened."

There was some silence. Morton waited patiently, arms raised. He had turned, and was facing the wall and the row of riot guns and pistols, and smiling at McGarvey, who stood irresolute in the middle distance.

Finally Jorgensen said: "I'm on parole, you know?"

"I know."

"I get caught hanging around a place where there's a job being pulled, and what happens to me? Back in. You know that."

"Sure. What were you doing there, Jorg?"

"I was parked there with a woman. A married woman, see? That made it that much worse. When we heard the noise we didn't know what the hell to do. I started the engine, but just as I was about to get going along comes a radio car. I stepped on the gas. Bumped another car on the way out over that bridge, and somebody popped at me."

"That was me."

"Thank God you're such a lousy shot, Mort."

"*Hmmmm.* As a matter of fact, I'm pretty good. But we won't argue about that now." Morton said.

"So anyway, I figured the best thing I could do was keep my mouth shut. Naturally I didn't expect all this."

"Naturally. You didn't see anybody run out of that house, Jorg?"

"I swear I didn't! I was too scared and excited to even look around."

Morton smiled grimly toward McGarvey and the weapon-lined wall. "Well, you're in a sweet spot right now. Better come out."

"If I do they'll beat hell out of me!" Jorgensen whined.

"If you don't," Morton reminded him, "they'll rush you and fill you full of lead."

"I swear I don't know any more'n I told you, Mort!"

"I believe you. But you better come out, anyway." Morton suggested.

"Will you keep 'em from beating me?"

"I'll do what I can. Chuck that gun out of the window, for God's sake, and let me put these arms down. They're getting tired."

4

MIDNIGHT ROUNDUP

IT WAS DINNER time, too late for the afternoon editions, when Morton and McGarvey emerged from the questions-and-answers chamber. Captain Montgomery came out a few minutes later, troubled, uncertain.

"What d'yuh think, Mort? After all, you're the one that got him."

"I'm going to eat. Keep the guy shut up, and tell the newspaper boys we're going to book him on a murder charge," Mort answered.

"But I don't think he is guilty!"

"I don't think he is either. Never have thought so. But I got a reason. Got a hunch I want to try out, with Garv here." Mort said.

"He sounds like he's telling the truth, to me. Even though he won't tell us the name of that woman he says he's with."

Morton shrugged. "Some guys got scruples, you know."

McGarvey growled: "Not some society guys. It takes a poor crook to be decent about it when he's fooling around with a woman. Didn't I hear you say we were going to eat, Mort?"

After the meal they returned to headquarters, where

Morton made five telephone calls. His manner was cheery, triumphant. He spoke to Campbell, Potter, Spofford, Carpenter and Mrs. Rawlins.

"Just wanted to tell you that we got the murderer!... Yeah.... You read about it, huh? Well, he was stubborn at first, but we went to work on him hard and now he's cracked wide open and confessed. Thought I'd tell you so's you'd understand why all the cops are leaving. We're calling 'em in, see?... No, it won't be necessary for you to come down for a look at him tonight. Tomorrow's plenty of time."

McGarvey said: "I don't get this at all."

"You will, sweetheart. We got lots of time for explaining. Come on."

HEART ISLAND, AFTER a turbulent twenty-four hours, was quiet again. The wavelets of Biscayne Bay stroked its shores, and the coco fronds rattled confidentially to the flowers and the impeccable lawns and drives. The five occupied houses were lighted, but they presented no activity. The moon shone down upon the scene not lavishly, as it had done the previous night, but intermittently, abolished occasionally, at irregular intervals, by sportive dark clouds.

A slamming door, the high note of a radio singer, sounded loud in that still place. Once an automobile entered, was driven into the garage back of Campbell's house. Periodically the new watchman from the Sweeney Agency made his rounds, whistling a little. He would walk across the plaza, up the roadway along the edge of the canal to the shore in front of the Rawlins house, then back around the yacht basin, up the other, similar roadway to the shore in front of the Hart Potter house. Then he would go back to his own little residence.

"He knows we're here, of course," Morton whispered, "but he's keeping the gate shut and acting just like he would on an ordinary night. I got two other Sweeney men hid in his house there, but I thought it best to have just us out here. If we had any more somebody'd be sure to get moving around, or light a cigarette or something."

They were near the yacht basin, near the plaza. Protected by the oleander bushes, they could see the road on each side of the canal, and they could see every one of the six houses.

"You still can't figure where you think these fellas are, huh?"

"I wouldn't even give a guess," Morton admitted. "The hunch just don't go that far, that's all. But I am convinced that they're in one of these houses, maybe hid in some secret room—somewheres where the servants wouldn't be likely to find them, anyway."

"Wouldn't it've been better to get search warrants?" Garv asked.

"Might be hard to get 'em in the first place. And in the second place, we'd come in for some awful hell if we did get them and then couldn't find anybody. Never knew anybody yet that liked to have his house searched, especially a millionaire."

"These society guys—"

"And besides, if we started searching it might tip them off, and they might make a break, all set. Or worse yet, they might decide to stay put and hold us off with artillery. You saw what a lot of trouble one no-account burglar like Jorgensen could make? And you can imagine what two professional killers could do in a place like this—with automatics and machine guns and all. Because these babies really are killers, Garv boy! Don't make any mistake about that!" Morton stated.

"Must be they look the part, huh? Or maybe they got records and are afraid of getting picked up if they just show their faces."

"Sure. But whoever it is got them here for the job, and is hiding them now—he could get them out easy enough by putting them on the floor of the back seat and driving past the watchman himself. Only he wouldn't have dared try that so long as the place was swarming with cops, the way it was a little while ago."

The lights of the Rawlins house went out. It was about ten thirty o'clock. Ernest Carpenter appeared, walking so quietly that they did not hear him until he was almost upon them. He strolled past. He was smoking a cigarette, and McGarvey's nose twitched regretfully.

After a time Carpenter went back. The lights in his house went out downstairs, and soon afterward the upstairs lights went out too. The Potter house was dark. Presently so was the Campbell house.

"Boy-oh-boy! I sure would like to have a smoke!" Garv whispered.

"Good training for you."

"I'll bet you're wishing you had one yourself."

"Sure I am. What the hell," Morton replied.

SOMETIMES THEY HEARD an automobile driven up to the gate they could not see, and they heard the watchman order somebody away. The general public was being kept out of Heart Island this night, and the gate, intended only as an ornament, was being put to practical use.

Spofford came out, with his wife, and they walked back and forth across the plaza. Spofford was smoking a cigar and its fragrance hung on the warm night air, causing McGarvey to stir restlessly. The strollers were talking in low, earnest tones. They walked to the gate, and presumably chatted for a time with the watchman—McGarvey and Morton couldn't see them now. They strolled back. Spofford tossed away his cigar, and McGarvey breathed a sigh of relief. Man and wife returned to their house.

Heart Island was very quiet. There were no more curious motorists. The watchman made his rounds, admirably ignoring the detectives among the oleanders. He still was whistling nothing in particular—whistling very low, as though out of respect for the still majesty of the night. The breeze had become smarter, more brisk. The moon was back of a broad mass of clouds.

"I'd give a week's pay for a butt," McGarvey whispered.

"Shut up! I think I hear something."

A shadow had appeared in the side yard by Hart Potter's house—a dim, blurred shadow—the shadow of a man crouching low, running. Another shadow followed it, and a third. They flitted ghost-like among the flower beds, making for the canal.

Morton cried: "Geez! I forgot all about that speedboat!" He started to run up the concrete retaining wall of the canal and McGarvey raced after him.

The three men saw them when they were about seventy-five yards away. One was standing in the stern, the other two were trying to start the engine. The whirr of the starter was the only sound in that still night.

The man in the stern started to shoot. The explosions were loud, sudden, harsh.

"The bushes, Garv!" Mort shouted.

Morton tore through the hibiscus hedge which lined the canal. It slowed him a little, but it put the hedge between him and the men in the speedboat. But McGarvey, Irish-mad, and aware only of the fact that somebody was starting something, continued to run along the wall.

Now two of the men in the boat were shooting. McGarvey fired back, twice.

The engine caught up with a terrific roar. The speedboat started for the end of the canal, for the open bay.

McGarvey, with his long legs, reached the boat as it was pulling away from the wall. He jumped into the cockpit, panting curses. He crashed full-length upon the floor.

Morton raced for the very end of the canal. It was the end of the hedge, too. The boat was picking up speed when it reached this point. Morton slapped the barrel of his pistol in his mouth, held it with his teeth—and jumped.

He struck a smooth, slippery, wooden surface. On hands and knees, he grasped an upright. Something hit him on the left shoulder. It felt like being hit with a club, and it almost threw him into the water.

THE MAN AT the wheel, now that the boat was clear of the canal, twisted it sharply to the right. Morton's left leg went overboard. His right knee was on the edge: he could feel the edge. Holding the upright with his left hand, he took the gun from his mouth and started to shoot.

It was a blind, crazy business. The moon abruptly floated

clear of the clouds, and Morton was able to see two figures. One held something shiny in front of him, and orange flame sprang from this. Morton couldn't even hear the sound of the shots—the engine was so loud.

Morton fired first at one figure, then at the other. He fired four shots.

The engine went dead. Amazingly, there was silence. Amazingly, the only sound was the soft slap of waves against the boat, a gentle swish as the boat's momentum carried it through the water. To Morton, his ears ringing with the explosions, it sounded like click-click-click, slow and regular.

Morton wriggled his way across the smooth top of the speedboat, always keeping the gun in front of him. He didn't dare get to his feet, or even to his knees. That would have meant moving the gun barrel.

Hart Potter was at the wheel. His face was white, and covered with sweat. One of the gunmen was draped over the low stern rail, his head and arms in the water. The other was kneeling on the floor, braced against the side, his arms over his belly, moaning horribly. On the floor was a third figure, which stirred as Morton dropped into the cockpit.

He jammed the pistol against the stirring figure.

"Hold it, punk, or your intestines get spilled," Morton rasped.

"Huh—hullo, Mort."

"Garv! You hurt, kid? Here, let me—"

"I—I'm aw—all right—"

The gunman kneeling on the floor moaned again, and toppled full-length. Morton picked up a pistol, deliberately hit the fellow behind the right ear. "You damn louse! You go blasting my sidekick, huh?"

He hit the man again. He wheeled upon Potter, who was motionless, almost fainting, at the wheel. "You, too, you damn louse! You're another damn louse!" He swung a right fist into Potter's face. Potter, hideously scared, crumbled without a sound. Morton knelt beside McGarvey.

"You all right, Garv boy? You O.K., kid? Listen, let me—"

"It—it's just my left arm, Mort. Hurts like hell."

Morton couldn't get the engine started, knowing nothing about speedboats. And Hart Potter, dazed, blubbering insanely between swollen lips, was of no help. It was not until Spofford came out in his cruiser, that they were able to get ashore. Heart Island was madly awake by that time, and swarmed with policemen and with millionaires in nightclothes. There was an ambulance, too.

"Never mind those worms," Morton cried. "Help me get Garv, here, up."

AT HEADQUARTERS, HART POTTER told everything unhesitatingly. His nerve was gone. He was hot, white, covered with sweat, dizzy, scarcely able to talk for the fear upon him.

"The one guy I didn't figure for the job," Morton growled. "How come you go hiring a couple of New York killers like that, anyway? What'd he ever done to you? Stepped on your lilies?"

"He stole my wife! I'd do it again, if I had the chance! He's the man who stole my wife! I only wish I'd killed him myself! All right—I don't care—put me in the electric chair! I don't give a damn! Put me in the electric chair!"

"We don't have to," Morton said. "You put yourself there, already, when you try murdering a guy by proxy, like they call it. If you wanted to murder a guy, why couldn't you do it yourself? These hot babies like Slavin and Nutsy Cort are bound to get you in trouble."

McGarvey was there, bandaged, not able to move easily, and with his left arm in a sling, but grinning. Morton turned to him.

"See—Potter hides the two bang-bang boys in his house, it being the night the servants were out, and then they cross the canal by means of the speedboat? See—it was swung right across the canal at that time, making a regular bridge, because it's just about as long as the canal is wide. He's fixed them with a plan of the Rawlins house, and after the job they breeze right across that boat-bridge again, and swing the boat around to where it was, and hide in some secret room in Potter's house. The only trouble he had was in trying to get rid of them. They had faces that a cop ought to know, because they're both notorious murderers and hot as hell, so he has to sneak them out the first chance he gets."

McGarvey, pursing his lips, looked disgusted. "Might have known there'd be another mattress affair behind the whole thing. These society people!"

THE CORPSE CLUE

They called Erskine "the man who never missed" for he'd masterminded more big crime ventures than any dozen other crooks— and never even been mugged or printed. But that was all before he ran up against those two amazing dicks from Miami H.Q. And a reputation for never slipping didn't impress Morton and McGarvey a bit— they'd just as soon ruin the successful career of an underworld world big shot as throw down on the pettiest punk operating.

1

J. EDISON ERSKINE

IN SOUTHWEST EIGHTH STREET, in a no-account little service station, the proprietor was pumping gas into the tank of a large and very dirty touring car—when a Ford squealed up the concrete apron. Now this was one of those paintless, disgraceful Fords, flappy of fender and unbelievably old. Its brake-lining was worn thin as tissue paper, and on this occasion it slipped altogether, so that the Ford collided noisily with the rear of the touring car.

The service-station man, understandingly furious, cursed at some length. Sore? Why the hell shouldn't he be sore when a crowd of low-down jellybeans, kiting around in a wreck that ought to have been barred from the public streets years ago, came smashing into his customer's car? Why didn't they take that lousy pile of tin to the junkyard, where it belonged? Where the hell did they think they were going?

One of the jellybeans managed to make himself heard above this profanity. He was pointing to a big blanket-covered bundle fastened to the trunk carrier of the touring car. The bundle might have contained camping equipment; but it didn't.

"Say, that guy's corn's leaking!"

"Corn?" The proprietor looked, saw liquid falling drop by drop to the concrete. "Say, that there ain't corn! Say, that looks like—"

Excited, forgetting about the accident, he fumbled with the bundle, pulled back one side of the strapped blanket. Then his face went perfectly white, and he turned away, leaned against a gasoline pump, and started to be sick.

For it wasn't a very pretty sight he'd seen. It was the body

McGarvey shot past the ratty one's head

of a gnarled, aged Oriental, and its face had been battered into a pulp. Even the jellybeans, who considered themselves very tough young men indeed, got a little green when they looked. And they were so stirred up about it, jellybeans and proprietor alike, that it was a full five minutes before any of them had sense enough to look around for the man who had been driving the touring car.

By that time, of course, the man was nowhere in sight. **MORTON POINTED TO** a man climbing into a taxicab. "There he is now." McGarvey put the police car into gear. He was shaking his head. "I can't understand, why worry about this guy when we got a real murder case. Geez! We don't get a murder every day!"

"We don't get a visitor like Erskine every day, either."

"What's so wonderful about him?" McGarvey asked scornfully.

"You don't have to try to scrape the cab's tail light… What's so wonderful about him? Why, he's smart. He's the smartest crook I ever hope to meet. When he pulls a job, it's perfect."

"Still, when we got a murder—"

"Here's how smart he is, Garv. He's probably lifted more than three million dollars worth of stuff in his time—jewelry and cash and bonds and everything else. And yet he's never stood in a line-up. He has no record, officially. He's never been mugged and printed," Morton informed him.

"Even so. What makes you think he ain't just here for a vacation?"

"Not this man. He's always working. He might take a month or more to box a job. He might spend hundreds of dollars on expenses. He might have a dozen men helping him—though most of them won't know what it's all about, until the last minute. But when he pulls it, it's pulled!"

Morton carefully put a cigar back into his mouth. "You can take my word for it, Garv: trouble always pops when that man's around. I swear if it wasn't for the fact that he's just got here this minute, I'd be tempted to think Erskine had something to do with killing that Jap, too."

"This guy's got you buncoed, Mort!"

"He's going into the Columbus. Pull up here, and wait for me."

"What about me coming along?"

"No. Erskine probably doesn't know you. You were still in harness when he was last down this way. He knew your old man and he'll probably know you soon enough, too. He gets to know everything, this guy!"

McGarvey shrugged huge shoulders. He slouched behind the wheel, trying to look bored. He could see nothing extraordinary about the man who was entering the Columbus Hotel—a mild-mannered, middle-aged fellow. Neatly, but by no means fashionably dressed, conservative in appearance, a typical business man. What else? He had a small, firm, brown mustache, and nose glasses. There were hundreds like him here, thousands.

"I won't be long," Morton promised.

McGarvey frowned at traffic. He would have preferred working on that murder case. You didn't get a murder case every day, and this one, so far, was a complete mystery. They hadn't been able to identify the car, or the missing driver, or even the victim himself. But McGarvey knew his partner. Morton might go around with a sad face, and he might keep things to himself, but he was the best detective in Florida. For that matter, McGarvey, who worshipped him, considered him the best detective in the whole world. He had been McGarvey's boyhood hero.

McGarvey himself, only twenty-three years old, shouldn't have been a detective yet; and he knew this. It was a matter of sentimentality. He owed his promotion to the memory of his father, who had been Morton's partner, Morton's side-kick, until a night club fight not so long ago. Morton and the elder McGarvey had stood side by side, shooting it out with a whole pack of gangsters from New

York. Two of the gangsters had been killed, three had been wounded. Morton had gone to the hospital for a month— and McGarvey, senior had gone to his grave.

AFTER THE FUNERAL they'd taken the dead man's son off radio patrol and made him a probationary detective. More, they had made him Morton's partner. "He's a good kid," Captain Montgomery had insisted. "He's strong and will- ing and all that. He may not be so bright, but he's strong and willing." Morton had merely grunted.

Morton was a hard man for a kid to work with. He rode young McGarvey constantly—not because he didn't like him, but because he did. He was afraid of spoiling the youngster.

Now Morton was returning. Tranquil, unhurried, he paused to light a fresh cigar. His face told nothing. It never told anything.

McGarvey asked: "What'd you learn?"

"Not a thing. Let's go back."

"He's just here on a vacation then?"

"So he says. But you take my word for it, Garv, we're going to have trouble in this town soon. I don't know what kind, and I don't know when it's going to break, or where. But we're going to have it!"

"Think we ought to have somebody tail him?"

"We're going to. Keaneley, nights. He's one of the young- est men on the staff, and maybe Erskine won't know him. And days, the other boy detective."

"The other—" McGarvey snapped a look at his partner, and almost scraped the fender of a Rolls-Royce. "Say, you don't mean me, do you?"

"Yes, I mean you."

"But hell, Mort! I don't want a job like that! I want some excitement!"

"Shouldn't have become a cop then." Morton smiled quietly. McGarvey was so boyish, so full of enthusiasm. It wasn't only his age. Probably he would always be this way. His father had been and often said: "Dullest work anybody ever did, this detective work. Except now and then...."

McGarvey spluttered all the way to headquarters, but Morton, cold and gray, paid him no attention.

"Just on the chance that Erskine might be fooled," Morton said, "I'm going to arrange to have you and Keaneley both put on the sick list."

"This guy Erskine can't be as smart as all that!"

"He's a whole lot smarter than you think. He's the one and only boss of anything he's involved in, but he usually has a flock of punks running around checking up on things for him and doing the dirty work. Naturally he's got me cased, because I almost did get the goods on him once, three years ago. But there's a faint chance that he won't know you and Keaneley."

"So I got to be sick? Well, if I'm sick I shouldn't have to work."

"You'll work, all right! You beat it right back to the Columbus, and you hang onto that guy like a mustard plaster."

"Aw hell, Mort! That's a lousy kind of a job, when there's a—"

"Goodbye."

Three hours later McGarvey telephoned. Erskine had taken a taxicab at the hotel, and had gone over to Miami Beach, to the Spanish Pavilion.

"Well, go on in after him!"

"Hell, Mort! You can't go in there unless you're going swimming, and I ain't got any trunks with me."

"Buy some! There's a shop there. Get yourself some pretty pants, and try to look like a *gigolo.*"

"What's new on that Jap killing?" McGarvey asked eagerly.

"Not a thing. Go to work. Goodbye."

THE SPANISH PAVILION is not exclusive. Any millionaire can patronize it. It has a restaurant, ordinary bath house which are called bath houses, fancy bath houses which are called cabanas, and its own private section of Miami Beach. It has, for that matter, its own private coconut palms, its own lifeguards, its own cigarette and lemonade girls. At certain hours of the afternoon it even has its own orchestra, and patrons may use their own dance floor. Patrons may also use the Atlantic ocean, in front, but very few of them go that far.

News photographers love the Spanish Pavilion. Actresses recline there in amazing bathing outfits; and the wives and mistresses of nationally-advertised products; and bank presidents, ambassadors, sometimes a celebrated novelist or two, all taking sun baths and trying to look bored. These people do not run away when men with cameras approach them.

McGarvey, two hundred and forty pounds of big bone and flat, hard muscle, in gabardine trunks and a giddy flannel robe, loafed on the white sand, trying, as Morton had suggested, to look like a *gigolo.* The photographers did not bother him. Neither did anybody else—except J. Edison Erskine.

A criminal, this Erskine? Why, a quieter, better behaved man would be hard to find! He sat gazing at the blue sea, at the creamy rollers, and he was almost blatantly inconspicuous on that beach where most of the bathers were trying to attract attention. He spoke to no one. Even the girl who sold lemonades from a basket-tray, and who clearly thought it part of her duty to keep unattached men from feeling lonesome, was not able to wring a smile from him. He bought a drink, and he nodded seriously, and paid her; but he seemed to give no attention to her talk.

It was a slow, warm afternoon, and the beach was looking its best. Elsewhere in the country hundreds of detectives, their overcoat collars turned up, drove or waded through snow and slush, cursing the day when they had elected to go into police work. Yet young McGarvey, decked out in blue and brown for which the City of Miami would pay a lot, was very, very unhappy.

"This is terrible, this place," he grumbled to Morton, over the telephone. "The people all talk like Englishmen."

"Never mind that! Where's Erskine?"

"Getting a massage. All afternoon he's been just sitting in the sand. Once he went in for a dip, and I figured at last I was going to get a chance to stretch myself, but all the guy did was fool around near the shore with a jerky little breast stroke, and pretty soon he came out again, so I had to come out after him."

"That's a shame. He talk to anybody?"

"Not a soul. And he didn't even look at me. I don't think he figures me for a shadow."

At headquarters, Morton cracked a soundless grin.

"Well, hang onto him. If he goes back to the hotel, Kean-eley will pick him up. If he don't, give me a ring."

"How's that Jap case coming?"

"Nothing."

"I'll be down there after Keaneley's relieved me, and—"

"You stay away from this place! You're on sickleave, remember!"

McGarvey sighed and said: "This is a hell of a life. After all, if this guy really is going to pull a job it'll probably be at the Beach, and that's none of our business, is it?"

"You do what you're told," said Morton, and hung up.

FOR FIVE DAYS the schedule didn't vary. McGarvey relieved Keaneley at 6 o'clock each morning in or near the Columbus Hotel. At 9:15, after breakfast at the hotel, J. Edison Erskine sallied forth, took a short stroll along Biscayne Boulevard, hailed a taxicab, and had himself driven out to the Spanish Pavilion. There he changed into a bathing suit and loafed all day on the sand, a tired business man relaxing. He lunched at the Pavilion, asking fussy questions like a man who must be careful about what he eats. He returned to his place on the beach. Once in the morning and once in the afternoon he took a brief, mildly hysterical swim. At 5 o'clock he had a message, dressed, and was driven back to his hotel—where Keaneley was waiting.

That was all. If this man was the greatest crook in the country, McGarvey reflected, he was the greatest actor too.

And Keaneley was reporting a night schedule just as uneventful. J. Edison Erskine would dine at the hotel, take a short walk, go to a movie, return to the hotel, retire.

"You go out on the beach, at least," Keaneley complained. "All I do is sit in this damn lobby all night!"

"It's lousy," agreed McGarvey. "I wish I knew what was happening on that murder case. Morton never tells a guy anything."

If McGarvey had ever supposed that he would like to be one of the idle rich, he was well rid of that idea now. He thought nothing was ever going to happen again.

Morton, on the other hand, was expecting almost anything to happen. Clean and gray and somber, he sat in his office seventeen out of every twenty-four hours. He sent and received telegrams, made long-distance calls, examined reports, shooed away newshawks. But most of the time he just sat there, staring at the ceiling, tapping his fingers upon the blotter, and wondering—wondering what he was missing.

They called Morton a genius. It was an exaggeration. But Morton was a mighty good detective, and he wanted a job done thoroughly. He was untiring, methodical, exact; yet when there were no clues he never hesitated to play his hunches. Just now he was convinced that in spite of the absence of anything to connect them, J. Edison Erskine was somehow mixed up with the death of that unidentified Japanese. He was trying to figure it out from that angle. He wasn't getting far; but he believed that this was because he was overlooking something obvious.

It was no mere hunch which prompted him to expect Erskine to strike, and strike hard, soon. He knew Erskine. He knew the absolute authority he had over such underlings as he found it necessary to use. Erskine was no small-timer, but neither was he a gangster. He picked his assistants cautiously and paid them well, different men for each new crime.

Erskine wouldn't overlook anything. But Morton was

overlooking something. What was it? He stared without expression at the ceiling, and tapped his fingers on the blotter, and wondered.

On the third day, young McGarvey had a slight addition to his regular telephoned report. "Things with the *gigolo* are just too thrilling for words! This damn supercrook of yours almost drowned today."

"I hope you took a poke at the mug who saved him?"

"I consider that a slur on the McGarvey name, sir."

"*You* did it? Why must *you* go round rescuing people? Haven't they got lifeguards in that dump?"

"Sure, but none of them were near at the time. The master mind was working that crazy breast stroke of his, when all of a sudden he swallowed a flock of water and began flapping his arms. I wasn't ten feet away. What else could I do? I couldn't let him sink!"

"I don't know why."

"Well anyway, I towed him in. It didn't amount to much. He wasn't more than fifteen or twenty feet from where you can touch bottom."

"So what did he say?"

"Oh, he thanked me all over the place. I told him to forget it. I think he was wondering whether he ought to offer me a reward or something, but he must have looked at my fancy pants and decided against it. Tough. Otherwise he didn't do a thing all day except to sit there in the sun, drinking lemonade, and eat lunch, and later get his rubdown. I'm calling from the Columbus lobby now. How long does this business have to go on, anyway? I'm going nuts!"

"It goes on until I call it off," Morton said. "Goodbye."

2

SNATCHED

ON THE FIFTH day, at about noon, the morgue people called Morton and demanded to know how much longer they were expected to keep that stiff. If the police weren't getting anywhere, why not plant the thing and get it over with?

Morton sighed: "O.K., go ahead."

"You can always dig it up, you know."

Morton returned to his contemplation of a singularly uninteresting ceiling. He told himself that he was a terrible detective. The world's worst. There was something right in front of him—and he couldn't see it. He could feel it, but he couldn't see it.

For no reason, the morgue man's reminder began to patter through his tired brain. "You can always dig it up, you know." He stiffened, looking at a wall instead of the ceiling. His fingers didn't tap any longer. He grabbed a telephone.

"Say, forget what I just told you, and hang on to that stiff! I'll be over."

Twenty minutes later, emerging from the morgue, he was wondering whether he'd thought of the right thing. It would take a day, maybe, to find out.

He was carrying a large, soft bundle. Laboriously—for Morton was getting on in years—he climbed into the department Chevrolet young McGarvey usually drove for him. Morton disliked driving. He particularly disliked it in Miami at the height of the season, when the streets were polychromatic with the license plates of every state in the union, and each individual driver had his own individual way of interpreting traffic rules.

Morton started the engine, and he was reaching for the emergency brake when a man climbed into the seat next to him.

This was a thin young man, a city man. He grinned crookedly from under a snap-brim hat. He said: "Hello."

Morton asked calmly: "What's the big idea?"

The young man was leaning close to him. "I don't know, cop. All I know is orders. You drive."

"Is that a gun you're poking into me?"

"Yeah, it's a gun. It goes off when you pull the trigger."

"It's against the law here to kidnap detective-sergeants on a one-way street. Maybe you're a tourist, and you didn't know that?"

"You drive, cop. I got everything set for me. If you don't behave, it goes blooey. And I got everything set. Not a chance of me getting caught at it."

"Sounds like my friend J. Edison Erskine."

"You drive out to Southwest Eighth, and then turn right."

McGARVEY WAS GETTING over the worst of his anger. He was beginning to think that this wasn't such a bad life after all, just lying here on your back watching the frothy wavelets. The sunshine was warm and full and rich. It seemed to sink right into your bones.

Twelve feet in front, J. Edison Erskine was lying on his right side. In exactly twenty minutes Erskine would turn over and lie on his left side. Twenty minutes after that he would roll upon his back. And twenty minutes after that he would get up, brush off sand and, followed by a lumbering McGarvey, stalk sedately to the edge of the Atlantic for his afternoon dip.

McGarvey yawned.

"Lemonade?"

He didn't want a lemonade, but he did want to chat with the girl. She was the only person in this place who didn't talk in a Harvard accent which gave McGarvey a pain.

"Didn't I used to see you down at South Beach?"

"You asked me that yesterday, and I told you I never been to South Beach. Lemonade?"

"Yeah, I'll take one. Well, you ought to go there. It'd be nice if you and I could go there some time."

She laughed, strolled on. McGarvey drank about half of the lemonade. He stretched out.

It really wasn't half bad. Those palms up there were pretty swell, the way they tossed back and forth in the breeze, like big upturned feather dusters. They tossed back and forth, not giving a hoot about anything. Back and forth... and the sunshine soaked right into you, like it was soaking clear into your bones....

Presently McGarvey sat up with a jerk.

He saw that J. Edison Erskine wasn't lying twelve feet in front of him. Erskine's beach robe wasn't there, either.

McGarvey ran down to the water's edge, looked around wildly. No sign of Erskine.

He ran back, went into a telephone booth. He was a little panicky now. He wished Morton were with him.

But Morton wasn't at headquarters! He had gone out about noon time, nobody knew where.

Then young McGarvey got really scared. Once again he searched the beach, the Pavilion itself, the pool, the dance floor and restaurant, the locker room. And he learned from a locker attendant that Erskine had dressed and departed almost an hour before.

"Get me a taxicab!" He started to peel off the fancy pants. "And I want a fast one, too!"

At the Columbus they reported that Mr. Erskine had checked out forty-five minutes before. No, they didn't know where he'd gone. He hadn't left any message for anybody, nor a forwarding address.

CAPTAIN MONTGOMERY TUT-TUTTED and pooh-poohed. "Don't you worry about Mort. He knows what he's doing. Maybe when you get to be his age, Garv, you will too. Though sometimes I doubt it."

"But where did he go?"

"Why ask me? He has charge of that Jap case, and he's been doing a lot of work on it, but he never opens his trap even to me. You know how he is." Montgomery tilted back, stared at the tan, anxious giant. "You better get out of here anyway, Garv. You're supposed to be sick."

They were, all of them, right when they figured McGarvey to be unburdened by too much brain. Yet possibly, as somebody had once suggested, the youngster wasn't quite as dumb as he looked—possibly working in the company of Morton helped.

Anyway, when after an almost sleepless night McGarvey learned that headquarters still had no word from Morton, he sat himself down to a breakfast of eggs and coffee and—thinking.

He had fallen asleep the previous afternoon. Why? Why do people fall asleep on beaches? Because of the sunshine. Yes, but the sun had shone just as hard each of the other four afternoons.

The lemonade!

Or, getting at it from another angle, how could Erskine plan things the way Morton said he did, with either Keaneley or McGarvey himself watching him all the time? With whom could Erskine have conferred? A few waiters, a couple of cashiers, a bus boy or two, a locker room attendant, a masseur—and the girl who sold lemonades!

It all pointed to her. Erskine had never appeared to pay her much attention, yet she had been in the habit of chattering to him when she sold or tried to sell him drinks. She hadn't been as sociable as all that with McGarvey—in spite of the fact that he had tipped her well, had invited her to go down to South Beach some day.

McGarvey, for all Montgomery's scowls, went into the office he shared with Morton. The older man, unlike his partner, kept a neat desk. Most of his papers were locked away. But there was one telegram under the blotter. It had arrived at noon the previous day, and obviously was an answer to a question put by Morton to one Anderson, of New York. McGarvey didn't know who Anderson was, but McGarvey's face became hot when he read the message—

ERSKINE EXCELLENT SWIMMER
AUSTRALIAN CRAWL.

So that was Erskine's idea of humor? McGarvey was beginning to understand, now, that Morton was right about this mild-mannered visitor. Morton was usually right about things. But where in hell was Morton?

McGARVEY WENT TO the Spanish Pavilion. He was esteemed a good customer there by this time, and the manager, smirking, had no objection to calling the lemonade girl out for him. She was getting into her costume just now—they were just opening the place—but he'd send her right back to the gentleman, of course!

She came, a hard little thing in a Majorcan peasant's dress, greeting McGarvey with a twisted, cautious smile.

"Listen." He stabbed an enormous forefinger at her. "That guy with the brown mustache and the nose glasses— the one with the purple beach robe—has he been around since four o'clock yesterday?"

"I haven't seen him. Why?"

"You know him pretty well, don't you?"

"Me know him? Why, no! Say, what is this, anyway?" she asked indignantly.

"You certainly used to stand and hand him a line, didn't you?"

"Well, I got a right to talk to a customer if I want, haven't I? He's a gentleman. He never made a pass at me. And he looked kind of lonesome sitting there."

McGarvey frowned. He wasn't good at this kind of thing, and he was wishing that Morton was here. McGarvey, when he got rattled, took refuge in bluster, which wasn't impressive, only loud.

"Listen, sister. I'm in a hurry, see? Now there was something in that lemonade you sold me yesterday, wasn't there?"

"Sure. Lemon juice. I suppose. And water—and sugar."

"Nothing else?"

"What d'you want for a quarter? A shot of Napoleon brandy?"

"Never mind the cracks." He flashed a badge. "Start talking that way and I'll take you somewhere where I can ask you right, see?"

As usual, his bullying didn't take. The girl only sneered.

"Flatfoot, if you was to pick me up I'd let out a squawk they could hear all the way up to the Surf Club. It'd be nice for you, huh? You ain't got a thing on me, and you ain't even operating in your own district. So get tough—go ahead, get tough!"

She glared a moment, then swung on her heel and flounced off.

But she'd been right. She was confident of herself, and her position. She knew she was being watched, knew that lawyers would appear promptly if it seemed that she was to be arrested. Besides, how could McGarvey even pick her up for questioning? He was in Miami Beach now, not the City of Miami. He wasn't a cop here, only a visitor. The girl had known that. But how had she known? She hadn't seen the badge long enough to read it.

McGarvey saw fire in the captain's eye as he entered headquarters.

Montgomery raged: "I thought I told you to keep out of here?"

"Sorry, Monty, but I'm worried about Mort," McGarvey countered.

"Well, stop worrying about him! Mort was getting out of tight places when you were still playing cowboys-and-Indians with the kids on the next block. He knows what he's doing, wherever he is."

"I know, but these people are smart—"

"And do you think Mort's dumb like you? Get out now, or I'll take you off the sick list and make you do some work for a change!"

But McGarvey didn't get out. He wandered disconsolate into his and Morton's office, and sat for a long time staring at Morton's desk. Finally he got a chisel from his own desk, and deliberately, silently, pried open drawers. Morton would bawl hell out of him for this—might even have him sent back on patrol duty—for Mort was fussy as any woman about his personal effects. Still, McGarvey considered it an emergency. McGarvey could have a hunch too. You can be dumb and still have hunches.

Reports, telegrams, precise little memos of telephone conversations. McGarvey frowned heavily over them.

THE JAPANESE, STILL unidentified, had been dead about two hours when found. A single bullet through the brain, fired at close range, had killed him. But the bruises and cuts on the Jap's face had been inflicted at least four or five hours before death. The Jap had been beaten into insensibility, permitted to lie for a time, then murdered. *Strong arm stuff not like Orientals,* Morton had noted. The car had not been traced. The plates had been issued to a fictitious personage, from a fictitious address in St. Augustine.

J. Edison Erskine, on his way south, had stopped at

Jacksonville over night. He had checked in at the Windsor Hotel a little before 6 o'clock Saturday evening. He hadn't been seen until he checked out the next morning at 8, to take a train south. He had taken that train.

However, another sheaf of reports showed that Erskine had received a telegram while passing through Savannah, before reaching Jacksonville. The telegram, obviously in code, had read—APPLESAUCE COOLING NOW. To which a to-be-called-for reply to Miami had been— GOOD LANDSCAPING.

Still another batch of memos and reports showed that a man answering the description of Erskine, though giving a different name, had chartered a fast plane at the Jacksonville Municipal Airport at 6:30 o'clock Saturday evening. He had flown to Miami, had instructed the pilot to refuel and to wait for him, and had departed in a taxicab. He had returned to the field four hours later, and had been flown back to Jacksonville. All this time he had not said an unnecessary word to the pilot or to any airport employee, and he had paid for everything, unhesitatingly, with cash.

Morton had noted—*Why all this? E. probably here when Jap beaten but could not have been when Jap killed. Careful to fix alibi. Somebody messed job of ditching stiff when ran out of gas. Now all hangs on. Who was Jap?*

McGarvey put everything away. The telephone rang. McGarvey listened.

"It's mostly *guano,* but the dirt's not local. Something like 'Glades muck, only it's not. Only thing I can figure it could be is the black stuff from Yucatan. Sounds crazy, doesn't it?"

McGarvey snapped: "It certainly does! Who's this, anyway?"

"Oh... Oh, isn't this Sergeant Morton?"

"No, this is his side-kick. Mort's out on a job."

"Oh. Well, this is Jefferies, at the Floridian Laboratories. Have him give me a ring when he comes in, won't you?"

"Wait a minute! He said for me to take a message if you called."

"He did? Well, tell Mort that the stuff's mostly fertilizer, mostly *guano,* but I can't figure the dirt at all. It's a rich, dried-out muck exactly the same composition as the soil from around the edges of the Caroni Swamp, in Yucatan. I just happen to know that because I was down there last winter, with the Wintergreen Expedition. I don't know whether that'll help him any."

"You mean," McGarvey guessed, "the stuff off that Jap?"

"Sure! The pants. Off the knees. Mort wanted an analysis."

McGarvey had a face painted thick with perplexity when he walked back into Montgomery's office.

"Are you still hanging around?" Captain Montgomery asked.

"It's mostly *guano*—"

"I think you're mostly *guano!* Get out of here!"

"Hey! that Jap was a gardener. Must have been. Mort had that much figured out when he did the powder act. Fertilizer and dirt on his knees. The dirt's from Mexico. Does that mean anything to you?"

"Nothing you'd say could possibly mean anything to me."

"Now listen, Monty: I'm worried. Ain't you going to send out a general alarm for Mort?"

"I've told you a hundred times Mort knows how to take care of himself. I send out an alarm and it might spoil some swell plan of his."

"But my God! you can't let a guy—"

"If we don't get some word from him by tonight I'll think it over. Meanwhile, since you're so anxious to find something to do, here's a cigar store that was busted into by some kids last night out at—"

"Not me! I'm a sick man!"

But he didn't look sick when he ran out of headquarters. His fists were clenched, his mouth was shut very tight, and there was murder in his eyes.

THE SNATCHING OF Morton had been beautifully executed. Even that veteran, soundless and watchful, had not been able to make a break. The thin man with the gun had leaned close to him, talking carelessly, but always tense, alert. He had given Morton no chance to stall the car, to cause a backfire, to precipitate even a minor accident. Three traffic policemen had hailed Morton. "Nod, and keep moving!" Morton had been told.

Once the man had said: "Take it slow at this next corner." Then another man had casually climbed into the car, into the back seat, and for the rest of the ride Morton had known that two guns covered him.

He had known that there were others behind, as well. In the mirror from time to time he had glimpsed a blue LaSalle, which kept close. Sometimes, when traffic was thick, it had even drawn alongside, blocking any chance Morton might have to scrape the fenders of some other car.

"Erskine sure does lay things out nice, doesn't he?" Morton said once.

"Keep driving, cop," was the answer.

Two hours later, handcuffed and very wet, he had faced six or seven men in a remote place, and had been told by a huge fellow with a cave man jaw that they desired to know just how far he'd got in his murder investigation. The contents of Morton's bundle—an old pair of trousers with the knees cut out—had seemed to disconcert them.

Morton had shrugged. "That's something I don't tell even my best friends."

"Listen, cop. You're where you can yell your head off if you want to, see? And nothing but alligators and rattle-snakes can hear you."

"Moccasins too," Morton had reminded. "Lots of them around here."

"All right, moccasins, too, then. But we got to get this dope."

"Why doesn't Erskine himself come out here and ask me?"

The big man had punched him in the mouth, then in the belly. It had knocked Morton down. But he hadn't moved, hadn't even blinked.

The rest of the men had edged a little closer.

"Do we go to work, or do you tell us what we want to know?"

"The boss is worried, huh? Well, he can stay that way." Morton was calm.

"I hope you can take it, cop."

"I guess I still can."

"I hope so, that's all. Because you're certainly going to get it!"

3

TAMIAMI TERROR TRAIL

THE SPANISH PAVILION closed whenever its patrons were ready to leave, but most of the beach attendants, including the lemonade girl, were off at 6 o'clock.

McGarvey was waiting for her, across the street, in his own battered Ford. He was tired. He'd been running around all day, visiting every place Morton might conceivably have visited. Montgomery might fume all he wished and postpone sending out a general alarm; but McGarvey had launched a general alarm of his own. He had asked every cop he met, in harness or in plainclothes. He had asked lots of other people. He had learned nothing except what they already knew—that Morton had left the morgue a little after 1 o'clock the previous afternoon, and that three traffic men remembered seeing him on Southwest Eighth Street, going west in the company of a thin, indefinite stranger. Nothing had seemed to be wrong with Morton then, the traffic cops said. He had acknowledged their salutes.

Southwest Eighth Street! It was in that street that the body of the Jap had been found, on an automobile pointed west!

Southwest Eighth Street is the Tamiami Trail. When it

leaves the east coast it goes across the state straight through the heart of the fabled Everglades. An amazing highway built largely by workmen operating from barges, it is practically one colossal bridge. Harsh and unbending, it cuts through as flat and dreary and dangerous an expanse of territory as is to be found anywhere in this country. A territory consisting of sawgrass, unseen water, poisonous reptiles, bottomless pits of muck and quicksand, water alleys which twist and turn or dead-end, and still, stinking pools in which alligators lurk. A white man lost there is a white man dead. The Seminoles alone, the only unconquered Indians in America, know the mysterious passages of the Everglades—and the Seminoles won't tell what they know.

The Tamiami Trail itself is alright, not a bad piece of pavement, lined by the conventional telephone poles and occasionally, though rarely, presenting an unexpected guide's hut, or even a dismal gas station. Yes, the Trail is all right. But on either side—

The girl came out, hurrying. McGarvey watched her as she walked down to Washington Avenue, saw her jump into a black roadster. He followed that roadster across the Venetian Causeway, down Biscayne Boulevard, out Flagler Street, until it stopped in front of an apartment house on Northwest Second, and the girl got out. The roadster turned left. McGarvey followed.

He might have guessed it! The roadster turned right, turned west, into Southwest Eighth Street.

Somewhere out near Coral Gables a blue LaSalle passed McGarvey and cut in front of the roadster. The roadster came alongside, and McGarvey could see that there was a conference. Then the roadster speeded up, made a right turn, disappeared. The blue LaSalle started to make a U-turn.

McGarvey deliberately rammed the LaSalle.

It wasn't a bad crash. Neither car had been going fast, and McGarvey had twisted his wheel in time to prevent a real head-on butting. He got out of his disgraceful Ford all complaints and curses. He stormed up to the ratty, steel-eyed little fellow in the LaSalle.

"Why the hell don't you look where you're going, you—"

"Say, wait a minute! Haul that piece of junk over the other side where it belongs, and then maybe I'll talk to you!"

But McGarvey was in the LaSalle now, in the front seat, and he was pressing a revolver against the ratty little man. He held the revolver in such a position that none of the other motorists could see it.

He said quietly: "Now what you do is to turn around an' go on out the way that roadster was going before you tipped him off about me."

"Say, what the hell—"

"Take it easy! I got a pal in trouble, and if you don't do what I say I'll turn this thing on. I mean it! I'm a cop, and this is my town, and if I kill you it's self defense. All right. Turn around."

THE LASALLE TURNED, started west on the Tamiami Trail. After a time the ratty little fellow asked from a corner of his mouth: "Where're we going. Hard-boiled?"

"I don't know. Where *are* we going?"

"I give up."

"A pal of mine is out this way somewheres," McGarvey said, "and I figured you'd know where it was."

"How should I know?"

"You'd better know," McGarvey said softly, "because otherwise I'll kill you."

The ratty fellow didn't seem to like this, but he didn't say anything. When they were clear of traffic McGarvey reached across him, took away an automatic. They were silent, driving fast.

"Is it near here?" asked McGarvey, at last.

"I don't know what you're talking about!"

"Because if it isn't, pretty soon I'll begin to get impatient, and when it gets good and dark I'll kill you and dump you out into the 'Glades. It's a swell place to dump bodies, out here. The alligators got little caves under the water that nobody can ever find, not even an Indian."

"I don't know what you're talking about!"

"I hope it's near here," McGarvey murmured.

Along the north side of the Trail, for a short distance, runs an odorous and unpleasant ditch known as the Tamiami Canal. Going west, they had it on the right. They were some fifteen minutes outside of the city when the ratty little driver did something McGarvey had not credited him with the guts to do. He picked a time when here were no cars in sight, and he swung the LaSalle violently to the right. It rose, shivered, squealed, and plunged, rolling, into the canal.

It went over on its right side, McGarvey's side. It didn't sink far. The rear wheels never got into the water at all, and McGarvey was wetted only up to his waist. But the suddenness of the move threw him forward, and his head struck a windshield upright. It stunned him. If the ratty little driver had been quickwitted he could have disarmed McGarvey in that moment. But the ratty little driver had other ideas.

Slowly, shaking his head, McGarvey climbed out of the car. He could see no sign of his late companion. But he was not seriously perturbed. There was no place for the driver to go except into the sawgrass, and for a man without hip boots this would be suicide.

The sun was gone. The moon, stolid and grave, in color an impressive orange-red, was barging up over the horizon, but not enough of it had appeared to be useful.

McGarvey gained the pavement, looked around. A hundred yards or so back in the direction of the city, he saw the dim outlines of a shack.

In back there was a pool, and the sawgrass was about thirty feet away, a black wall some five feet high, punctured by two water-lead entrances. There was a *pirogue,* an Indian dugout, with a pole in it; and McGarvey saw, by getting down on his hands and knees, that another *pirogue* had been here a few minutes earlier. Water was even now oozing back into the mark it had left in the mud.

Far away, to the west, he could hear the dull, muffled hum of an automobile engine. Ahead, somewhere, he heard another sound. He listened very carefully for a moment; and then he sprang into the dugout, grabbed the pole, and started for the water-lead on the left.

McGARVEY WAS NO stranger to the Everglades. He had traveled through parts of them on fishing trips, and he had often poled canoes like this one. Still, it gave even McGarvey a creepy feeling to push off into that vast aquatic wilderness in pursuit of a shushing sound which had seemed to be on the left.

If he had heard wrong, he would never come back. The water-lead might go anywhere at all. He might pursue it all night, all the next day—pursue it, and the leads which branched from it, until he dropped from exhaustion. That is, if he had heard wrongly.

The lead forked. McGarvey, his pole held high, listened again. He took the left fork.

He poled very hard, but without making a sound. He crossed several pools. The moon was getting higher now, and paler, and more useful if less lovely, and so he was able to make out the places where the lead continued.

He came upon the other *pirogue* rather suddenly. It was on the far side of an exceptionally big pool, a veritable lake, and, just as McGarvey's *pirogue* burst into this pool, the moon seemed to leap clear of the horizon and to suddenly shed her fullest and finest silver light. It was as though a stage electrician had removed an amber gelatine from some spotlight. There were two men in the pirogue—the ratty little fellow was in the bow, sitting down. A bulky, massive man in a floppy felt hat, was poling.

McGarvey bellowed: "Stop!"

He saw them both turn, saw the ratty fellow make a gesture to the man in the stern. Then the *pirogue* started for a blind water-lead. If it reached that it would be lost. Lost forever, as far as McGarvey was concerned. And he would be lost too. The big man in the floppy hat assuredly was a guide, and without him McGarvey couldn't hope to get back to the highway.

So McGarvey didn't do any further shouting. He drew the automatic and started to shoot.

He didn't shoot high, either. Or low.

The *pirogue* drifted to a stop. The big man dropped his pole, raised his arms.

"Hold it there!" McGarvey commanded.

Poling with one hand, awkwardly, and with his right fist holding the gun, McGarvey approached the other dugout. The ratty little fellow had been hit twice in the left arm and shoulder, and he was cursing softly, pauselessly. The big man had no expression. He might have been frightened, but he didn't show it. He was an Indian, as McGarvey had guessed.

"What's the hurry? Take me along, why don't you?" McGarvey was calm but very angry.

HALF AN HOUR later they came in sight of a Seminole hut on a little island which contained also a cabbage palm, a clump of palmettos, a lot of pickerel weed, and nobody knows how many reptiles and insects of malicious intent. It was a platform on poles, two feet above the slimy earth. The roof was palmetto-thatched, on the walls were hung deerskins.

McGarvey whispered "Go it easy, big boy. You too, punk."

The Indian was obedient. But the ratty little fellow, when they got within ten feet of the shore, yelled: "Joe! Joe! Look out!"

A deerskin was pushed aside, and a big man in overalls and rubber boots jumped to the ground. He held a rifle, which he raised to his shoulder. McGarvey shot him through the heart.

Another deerskin moved. There was an explosion, and a second man tumbled out of the hut as though propelled by some force behind him. He held an automatic, and he had fired this, but the shot had plopped harmlessly into the water.

This man landed on hands an knees. He raised his automatic, aiming at McGarvey. McGarvey fired three times at him, and the man slithered quietly back into the muck.

Then silence. The moon, getting smaller and brighter and higher all the time, gazed in disapproval at this excitement. Nobody moved.

From inside the hut, weakly: "O.K., Garv. That's all there is."

"Mort!"

Sergeant Morton's lips were huge, puffed, bloody. His left eye was closed. His cheekbones were swollen. There was no part of his face which was not covered by angry bruises. In front of him, his wrists were handcuffed. He gestured toward the man with the pistol.

"He had a bead on you and he was just about to let fly when I clouted him with the cuffs here. Incidentally, he's the one's got the key for these things. You might let a man loose."

"Mort! Look at your face!"

"I can't, thank God." Morton was examining his late jailers. "Too bad you had to kill these lice, at that. I wanted them to tell me things. Erskine's pulling some kind of a big job tonight—I could find out that much, from the way they talked, but I couldn't find out what it's going to be."

From the dugout: "And you ain't likely to find out, either!"

Morton, cold and impersonal as always, stared at the ratty little fellow. He nodded slowly; then spoke.

"So you know, huh? Well, that's just ducky. So you'll tell us."

"So you can go do things to yourself!"

Morton moved his lower jaw back and forth. "All right. We'll find out anyway. And you can stay here while we do."

"Hey, wait a minute! You can't leave me in this place!" Panic had the ratty one. "The mosquitos'll suck all the blood—all my blood—"

"Oh, you can swat them. They're not bad. Only don't try swatting the snakes, when they come at you. Or the alligators."

The ratty little fellow might have taken a beating. He was tough. But being left alone on a poisonous islet in the middle of nowhere, with two corpses—that was something different.

McGarvey hauled him out of the canoe as though he'd been a sack of potatoes, and dumped him into the slime. The little fellow didn't stir, but he stared up wildly out of the corners of his eyes. Already he was feeling the soundless, clammy caress of the snakes, and seeing the monstrous jaws of alligators.

"I can't yet understand why they didn't kill me," Morton said, as he limped across the clearing to the dugout. "There were times when I wished they would. Must be Erskine forgot to give them definite orders."

McGarvey noticed the limp, noticed for the first time that his partner's right foot was bare.

"Good God! You don't mean to tell me they—"

"It's all right. Hurt like hell when they did it, but there's no sense yapping about it now. It's all on the bottom, and as a matter of fact this mud feels kind of good against it. Come on."

The ratty little fellow screamed: "Listen!"

"Why?" asked Morton.

"Listen, I'll tell you where that job's going to be!"

"Sure. You'll lie to us to try to get off this place."

"I won't lie!" He coughed. His face was utterly white. "You take me away and I'll tell you where it's going to be. They got everything set. It's—it starts at nine o'clock."

HE COUGHED AGAIN—AND blood slipped from the corners of his mouth. His eyes had a glazed, sticky look.

"It's at—it's going to be—"

McGarvey, suddenly alarmed, knelt close to him.

"He must have got it when the automobile crashed, Mort! From the steering wheel. Must have busted a couple of ribs and they pushed through."

Morton said: "All right, punk. Spill, and we'll take you along. But as sure as hell, if we find out you were lying we'll bring you back here and leave you—the way you are now."

The lips moved a little. McGarvey leaned very close.

"Nine—nine o'clock—it's at—it's—"

There was one last little cough, and the mouth stayed open. The eyes stayed open too. But the blood ceased to trickle down the chin. After a time McGarvey rose, frowning.

"Hell, Mort, he's dead."

"Hell," said Morton. He fumbled in a pocket, drew out two cigars badly crushed, and scowled at them as though he resented their existence. He threw them into the water.

The Seminole stood motionless, a statue.

"You know, Garv, I think I must be a lousy detective."

"You are. You never tell a guy anything."

"I've been missing something right along, and I can't think what it is. Something about that Jap. He was a clean little devil, spick and span. I had them pare his nails and cut off some of his hair, and I even had them scrape out the inside of his nose and the wax from his ears. We didn't find a thing."

"Oh, that reminds me! Jefferies called up, from the Floridian Laboratories, and he said the stuff on the knees was mostly *guano*."

"I knew that already."

"But there was dirt too, and the only place he could figure it came from was some swamp in Yucatan. Sounds goofy, but that's what he said."

"Yucatan?"

"That's what he said. Yucatan. I can't figger it at all."

Morton put both hands into his pockets, and for the space of two full minutes he gazed past the Seminole at the far-stretching wasteland. Once he blinked. Otherwise he might have been a figure in wax.

Then he jerked into action, limped to the dugout.

"You, big chief! Start making that pole work like you never worked it before! Act like a ghost was chasing you! Never mind these stiffs! They can get picked up later!"

"Mort, what's it all about?"

"And as for you, you damn *gigolo*, grab that other pole and put that beef of yours behind it!"

"But it's almost—it's practically nine o'clock now."

"Push! It'll take 'em close to an hour, probably. And we might get there before they're finished. Now listen. When we reach the Trail, you stop the first car that comes along if you have to lie out across the middle of the pavement to do it! Understand?"

"I don't understand anything, yet."

"You don't have to understand anything yet. You push!"

4

MANSION MURDERS

J. EDISON ERSKINE stood in the great entrance hall of one of the most celebrated mansions in the world, which was set in the middle of one of the most celebrated private parks in the world. Even east-coast Floridians, sophisticated in the matter of multi-millionaires' estates, mentioned the Hallwell place with breath never less than bated. For it represented not only incalculable wealth, which is always impressive, but a wealth varied and colorful, exotic, spectacular. It was an Eden, self-contained. The fabulous Indies had contributed to it, and English castles, Germanic monasteries, French *châteaux,* the palaces of, once opulent, Moorish potentates, the studios of, once impecunious, Italian painters. The result, if occasionally confusing, was indisputably magnificent. And J. Edison Erskine, looking around, was pleased with himself and his work.

For Erskine, for the hour, was the master of this whole stupendous establishment. More, he was feeling the thrill of a great general as carefully laid battle plans work out perfectly beneath his gaze. He was Napoleon. But his battalions were criminals. They executed, he commanded.

He looked like a minor pillar of society. With his glittering nose-glasses, his mustache, his modest, severe business suit. He might have been the second-vice-president-in-charge-of-production of some sizable corporation. He was almost poetically prosaic—in appearance.

His men, before going out to the truck, paused in front of him, and he checked their burdens of silverware, tapestries, paintings, pieces of antique furniture. He made a quick estimate of each article, and with a silver pencil, on a neat, business-like pad, he jotted down a brief description.

His wrist watch told him it was 9:32. Within twenty minutes he should have this place stripped of its treasures. He expected them to be worth at least a million dollars, even at thieves' prices. Of this he would take fully two-thirds. He deserved it. For hadn't he conceived the job, boxed it, done all the real executive work? He had hired these petty criminals as a shipper hires longshore-men. They were guaranteed so much, plus a bonus if all went well. Some of them were Hallwell employees, some were outsiders. Many of them did not know one another, and might never meet. J. Edison Erskine was the tie that bound them.

This was what he loved; to stand here in the center of things, quietly directing the checking, feeling everything go like well-oiled machinery. He had no desire to be anything so vulgar as a gang leader, or an outlaw might do. It was possible that he would never see any of these subordinates again. He didn't care. He would use them, pay them and leave them. He was not even worried about the chance that some of them might be caught and confess. His alibi, as always, was fixed. Seven well-bribed persons were ready to testify that he was at this very moment in a fishing camp on Soldier Key, miles and miles away.

A man in a greasy monkey-suit approached, almost saluted. "One of those guards got fresh and the boys had to slug—"

"Yes?"

"It looks like he's croaked."

"All right. Now look: I want you and Washert to take down that gray mural you see up there. Handle it like eggshell china! It may look like a nightmare, but it happens to be worth a lot of money."

J. Edison Erskine walked with a brisk, exact step into the dining room. The sideboards there stood open, the walls were bare, but the floor was littered with squirming, trussed servants—servants who had not been considered important enough to take in on this job, or who had been esteemed over-honest. Their eyes were bandaged. None of them had, at any time, glimpsed J. Edison Erskine himself.

He walked into another room, a butler's pantry. There lay Silas Hallwell and his wife, and their seventeen-year-old daughter, all tied and bandaged and taped like the servants. Like the servants, too, they had never seen Erskine. They were in evening clothes, somewhat torn. The women's jewelry, and Hallwell's diamond studs and links, together with the rest of the contents of the Hallwell safe, were in the side pockets of J. Edison Erskine's automobile. Erskine believed the stuff to be worth fully $800,000, retail.

Out in the entrance hall again, he jotted a few more items in his pad. He glanced at his watch. 9:39. The detective employed by the agency which patrolled this and several neighboring estates, would make his usual appear-

ance at some time between 9:55 and 10:10. Erskine hoped
to be finished before he came. But it didn't matter, really.
The man could be blackjacked.

"Don't you think it's about time you tied me up?"

JORGENSEN, THE SUPERINTENDENT of the estate, was
not a professional criminal, merely a hitherto substantial
workingman who had succumbed to big temptation; and
now he was badly frightened. His little blue eyes moved
back and forth. He kept running fingers through his thin
yellow hair.

Jorgensen had been Erskine's first contact, and through-
out the preliminary period he had done much of the field
work. He was to split fifty-fifty with Erskine. At least, that
was the agreement.

"Yes. Make it in the kitchen, I guess."

"Why not out here? It would look as if I—"

"The kitchen would be best," Erskine said coldly.

Jorgensen shifted uneasily, moving those blue eyes back
and forth. He couldn't understand this Napoleonic chief
who awed him.

"Is—is everything going to be all right?"

"Certainly," said Erskine. "If you hadn't misjudged
that Jap, there wouldn't have been a suggestion of a hitch
anywhere."

"He fooled me! I didn't think he could understand
enough English to know what Sanderson and I were
talking about, but he did!"

"You should never trust anybody," said J. Edison Erskine.

"He's only been here a little while. They engaged him to
build a Japanese garden back beyond the swimming pool.

I don't know where he got all that damn loyalty from! But he meant it. He was ready to go to the police."

"All right. He's fixed now, anyway. Get into the kitchen."

Jorgensen walked away jerkily, nervously, still glancing left and right, right and left. Erskine stood there frowning a little.

Even a master slips sometimes. He had slipped on that Jap, and he knew it. That man Morton! Erskine should have disposed of him somehow before starting on this job. He should have known a smart cop when he saw one. Morton had crossed his path before.

For a time there, though, it had been just funny. J. Edison Erskine had been vastly amused by the two youngsters assigned to shadow him, and particularly by the bigger one, McGarvey. It had been grand to sit on the beach day after sunny day, getting a beautiful tan, and all the while, by means of Stella, supervising preparations for what would prove the greatest house-breaking in the history of crime— while the good McGarvey, blissfully supposing that he looked like a Spanish Pavilion *habitué*, had sat near him.

Funniest of all had been getting McGarvey to swim him in! Pretending to be in distress, a drowning man! The fool cop had looked so excited, had made such a show of modest heroism after the event!

"Tell the boys to go through the servant's quarters too," he instructed a man near him. "Even the ones working with us. I want it to look like a thorough job, to cover them up." Then he went into the kitchen.

Tying and taping Jorgensen was the only manual work he had done, and he did it well. When he was finished he drew a small automatic, and from another pocket a silencer. He started to screw the silencer on the muzzle of the automatic.

"You did good work at that, Jorgensen, for a beginner. But you'd never make a first-class crook. Too nervous. I hate to have to kill you, but I can't afford to let the cops get at you. I don't think you could take it. And you see, you're really the only one in the whole outfit who has enough on me to hang me. So…"

He had the silencer adjusted to his satisfaction. He held the gun at arm's length, shook it hard, nodded.

"And besides, I want your split."

JORGENSEN, UNABLE TO speak, scarcely able to move, thumped his heels on the floor, arched his back. Stark terror was in those blue eyes of his, bulging like blue pingpong balls. His face was dark red, almost purple from strain. Jorgensen hadn't expected this!

J. Edison Erskine aimed carefully at the space between the blue pingpong balls. Jorgensen, defeated, or paralyzed by fear, was motionless now. Erskine fired twice. Then he leaned over and shook the body, felt the heart, the pulse. He straightened, satisfied. He unscrewed the silencer and put it back into a trouser pocket, and the automatic, after inserting a couple of loose cartridges into the clip, he put into a side coat pocket. He left the kitchen without a backward glance.

It was 9:44.

Exasperating, too, thought J. Edison Erskine, that the boys hadn't been able to get Morton to talk. That man must have been tough as well as smart. Well, he was dead now. Clarky Lewis had been directed to take the kill order out to the hut, after first taking Stella home from the Span-

ish Pavilion. Clarky would pick up the two men left on
the island to guard Morton, and then those three were to
be important factors in the final fulfillment of the night's
plan—the concealing of the treasure truck. J. Edison
Erskine had it all figured out.

Somebody cried: "There's a car coming up the drive!"

It didn't seem possible. Erskine hurried to a front
window. Yes, there was a car coming up the winding, mile-
long drive. A small car. It got closer. A truck! A florist's
delivery truck!

Erskine, who had arranged to have both entrances
guarded, couldn't understand how this car had got into
the estate. He couldn't know, of course, that it had not come
by an entrance—that it had crashed through a boxwood
hedge from an adjacent estate and been driven across rolling lawn to the main drive. But Erskine acted fast.

"You! You footman, whatever your name is! Go out and
tell him nobody's home. If he has anything to deliver, take
it and sign a receipt. But don't let the man get out! The rest
of you stay hidden."

Erskine had a small black automatic in each hand now,
but in spite of this fact he still looked like a respectable
business man. The others were drawing pistols. There were
nine of them altogether, less than half the number involved
in the whole plot.

The florist's truck stopped at the side entrance, directly
in back of the big truck in which the Hallwell treasures
were to be removed.

The footman, stiff and proper, stood on the lowest step.
He leaned far over, peering into the front seat, saying
something.

It was very quiet in that enormous house.

J. Edison Erskine watched with narrowed eyes. His thumbs simultaneously clicked off the safeties of the two pistols he held. Very quietly he moved toward the front door, though he never lost sight of the footman through a series of windows. Nobody noticed his retreat.

Always J. Edison Erskine thought first of J. Edison Erskine. He might use twenty men in the commission of a crime, but only one of these was of any real importance to him, and that was the leader. Tonight his own fast roadster was in front of the house, the door open, the engine running; and in the side pockets were the Hallwell jewels.

THE FOOTMAN LEANED a little closer. They couldn't hear what he was saying, but from the way he moved his arms they gathered that he was having an argument with somebody in the truck. Suddenly he turned, as though to run back to the house. A long arm reached out, a hand grabbed the footman's coat, and the footman's head and shoulders, together with a good part of his body, disappeared inside the truck. He started to yell something—and then there was silence.

Silence only for an instant. The footman, limp, was shoved backward and fell upon the steps. A bellowing giant with a revolver in one hand, an automatic in the other, leapt from the truck and started up the steps. And then everybody began to shoot at once.

Of course it had been McGarvey's fault. McGarvey had been just twitchy for a fight, jumpy, bubbling with Irishness. These were the mugs who'd given old Mort that shellacking! These mugs were the ones who'd burned Mort's foot! He'd show them!

Morton would have stalled. He wished only to block the drive against the departure of the big truck, until the riot squad arrived from headquarters. There would be plenty of time for shooting then. Or maybe shooting wouldn't even be necessary, if Montgomery brought enough men.

But McGarvey had lost his head again. He had started to bluster, and this alarmed the footman. Then there had been nothing to do but sock the footman in the jaw, which McGarvey had done.

Like a crazy man he charged up the steps, and the whole front of the house seemed to explode. But he had fool's luck. Lead whistled all around him. Lead tugged at his sleeve, ripped holes through the loose of his trousers, knocked his hat off; but, miraculously, the bulk of McGarvey himself was untouched.

Yet it sobered him a little—it was enough to sober anybody—and he threw himself sideways behind a large ornamental stone vase. A few small chunks of that vase violently quit the parent body, and as though by an abrupt trick of magic one side and the top became ludicrously chipped and pitted. But it held together. McGarvey wriggled into some bushes.

Morton? Morton knew his J. Edison Erskine, and was thinking of that strategist's possible line of retreat. Morton left the truck by the far side. No lead came his way, and he was tolerably certain that the men in the house had not seen him, did not even know of his existence. McGarvey, big McGarvey, had been behind the wheel, on the side toward the house, and it was at him that they were shooting.

Morton, aiming carefully, put one bullet into each of

the huge rear tires of the treasure truck. They burst with a terrible roar; but this sound was lost in the volley which chased McGarvey behind the vase.

The truck, at least, wouldn't go far now!

There was a chilling silence. Men were running back and forth inside the house, taking care, however, to keep away from the windows; but there were no shots meant for Mort. Apparently they still hadn't seen Morton. They knew where McGarvey was lying, but they couldn't reach him with bullets because of the protection of the stone vase and the thick retaining wall at the end of the steps. They could not reach the treasure truck without killing him first, and they could only kill him by rushing him. They must have known, as Morton knew, that McGarvey was ready for a rush.

The footman, white-faced, his eyes closed, still lay sprawled across the three lowest steps. McGarvey packed a terrific wallop in that big right hand of his. He was, as Montgomery had pointed out, strong and willing.

Morton heard a car door slam, heard an engine roar. Erskine! It was at the front of the house, out of sight, but not thirty feet from where Morton crouched. He broke cover, started to run for the corner of the house. J. Edison Erskine was the man he'd come to get, and J. Edison was quitting the party.

HOW HE HAPPENED to see the man on the balcony he could never explain. He must have sensed his presence.

The balcony was on the second floor, partly above the side entrance. The man was leaning far over the railing, and was aiming a pistol at the space beyond the retaining wall at the side of the steps. From that position he was able to get a line of McGarvey, who did not see him. He could shoot over the wall. He was about to do precisely that.

Morton had been running hard. He stopped so short that he went to his knees. But he snapped two shots balconyward before he slammed against the earth.

The man left the balcony in a leisurely, even a graceful manner. It was like a slow-motion picture of a fancy diver. Only the man didn't perform a complete turn. He turned half-way, in the air, and landed upon his back at the head of the steps. It made a nasty sound.

Now those in the house became aware of Morton. As he sprang back for the cover of the truck there was a blast of gunfire. Something whammed his left leg, whirling him completely around and throwing him flat. But he landed behind the protection of the truck.

"Back against the wall, Garv! Back against the wall!" He kept yelling this, hoping that McGarvey would hear between shots. "Back against the wall! They can get you from that balcony!"

Too late now to go after J. Edison Erskine. Too late to shoot at rear tires from the corner of the house, as Morton had planned to do. He heard the engine rear away, then come nearer. There was no back drive out of the Hallwell estate: the drive encircled the house, joined the main drive at the side, branched further down toward the highway. Erskine would have his choice of the main drive or the service drive, after he got around the house.

The car spurted into sight. It was going very fast, without lights. When Morton first saw it, it was about thirty feet from where he lay. Deliberately, methodically, he started shooting at it.

Somebody in the house was screaming: "He's gettin' away with the jools! He's gettin' away with the jools!" Erskine's hired help were learning the character of their master.

Sheer luck. The third bullet caught a tire. The car lurched, shrieked protestingly upon gravel. It spun around twice and smashed sidewise into a tree. Erskine sprang out, and started to run along the edge of the drive. He was limping badly.

Morton dropped an empty revolver, shifted the automatic to his right hand, emptied the clip at Erskine's legs.

Morton wasn't alone. They were all shooting at Erskine now. The master crook, the man who never missed, sprang right off his feet, as though somebody had rammed him with a pole in the small of the back. He fell heavily upon his face. Even then the angry men in the house didn't stop shooting at him, and his body jerked again and again under the impact of bullets.

Who killed J. Edison Erskine nobody was ever to know. Afterward they took no less then seventeen slugs out of his corpse. Seventeen slugs of lead, which the ballistic experts proved had been fired from five different pistols.

"Back against the wall, Garv!"

But McGarvey yelled: "They're making a break out the back way! I can hear them! I'm going around!"

"Don't go there, you damn fool! Let 'em break!"

Morton would have run after him, pulled him back—only Morton couldn't. With his elbows, mostly, he dragged himself as high as the running board. He could do no more. He was cursing steadily, softly, without heat. He didn't even stop cursing when he heard the siren, saw the lights of the car from headquarters.

As for McGarvey, he was a fool to the last. He went chasing unimportant cogs of the smashed Erskine machine through all sorts of shrubbery. The wonder was that one of Montgomery's men, who soon swarmed all over the place, didn't plug him by mistake.

Yet McGarvey wasn't touched! He hadn't been so much as grazed by any bullets! And he came back singing *Just a Gigolo.*

WHEN McGARVEY SAW Morton sitting on the running board, surrounded by reserves, he grinned. Hands on hips he stood there.

"Well, I guess your master mind won't try pulling any more jobs in this town, huh, keed?"

Montgomery approached, panting, cursing. "Who was it phoned me, anyway?"

"The guy who drove that florist's truck that we stopped on the Trail," McGarvey explained. "We had him bring us in, but we were running pretty close to Erskine's schedule and Mort didn't think we ought to telephone ourselves. So we dumped the guy out and told him to call, and we raced on here, hoping to hold 'em in until you guys came."

"I still can't understand how you knew to come here."

"Neither can I. Mort's the boy who doped that out. Ask him."

"The Jap," Morton muttered. He still was sitting on the running board, his elbows on his knees. He looked sick. "Clothes were clean, but there was fertilizer ground into the pants at the knees, so I knew he was a gardener. I had the boys checking up on possible missing Japanese gardeners, but it might have taken them a week to find out anything that way—which might have been too late. So then I thought maybe Jefferies could analyze the dirt that was mixed in with the fertilizer. There wasn't much of it, but Jefferies is smart that way, and he's been studying that kind of thing for years."

McGarvey cried: "But he said it came from Yucatan!"

"Sure. Don't you remember reading, eight or nine years ago, how Hallwell was rebuilding some of his terraces and he decided to have some special earth put in? His head gardener then was a Mexican—of all funny things for a gardener to be—and he sold Hallwell the idea of import-ing swamp muck from Yucatan. It cost a couple of hundred thousand. But what'd that mean to Hallwell? Chartered a whole ship, and it made five trips. The papers were full of it at the time."

"Now I call that brains," breathed McGarvey—an awed young man.

Morton grunted. "Had to use a little brains, working against a guy like Erskine. He must have had men watch-ing me all the time, wondering whether I was going to get enough to spoil his big job. And when he found out somehow, or guessed, that I'd caught up on what I'd been overlooking all the time—he snatched me. He had that hut out in the Everglades as a sort of emergency hideout. He thought of everything, that man! Only thing is, he used to get such elaborate plans that if any one little thing went wrong, when he wasn't there to supervise, then the whole works might come crashing down. This time it happened to be that a punk assigned to get rid of the Jap's body let himself run short of gas. It just goes to show."

McGarvey stepped closer, squinting. "Say, what're you sitting there like that for, Mort?"

"Because I can't stand up, you halfwit!"

"Hell, Mort, I'm sorry! I forgot about that foot!"

"It's the other side now. I caught something there." He leaned against the side of the car, and shut his eyes. "So I'm going to find me a nice quiet hospital somewhere, and then I'm going to—"

"Geez, he's passed out!" McGarvey yelled.

"No, I haven't. I'm just dreaming about that hospital, that's all."

"Hell, Mort! You've been stopping everything on this party! You ought to be more careful about the way you rush into things!"

"You talk too much, Garv. You're disturbing my dream. Go away. You got no business around here anyway. You're on sick leave."

THE CARRION CLUE

McGarvey leaned to brawn rather than brains all right, but he had keen eyes set in his head—even if it was thick. So when the buzzards showed him the way to that carrion clue he didn't need to look twice. And after he'd told his partner where the bodies lay it was pie for Morton to add two to two to get the total of the kill sum.

1

A CORPSE IS MURDERED

IT WAS A quiet thoroughfare. Mango trees blocked the warm Florida moonlight; the houses were set far back, and surrounded by shrubbery; and there was seldom any traffic after dark. In consequence, the spot was much favored by motorists who wished to indulge in kisses and soft words and things like that. If it had been sufficiently celebrated, somebody would have entitled it Lover's Lane. Actually its name was LaConcha Road.

It had seen some curious couples in its day—or its night—but the couple in the blue Ford was the strangest yet.

From a little distance they were blurred figures under the shadows. But when you got close you saw that the one behind the wheel was a man in his fifties, a square, somber, gray man who looked like a tired bishop. His companion was huge and ungainly, and wore an organdy dress, white, stiffly starched, and a large, pink picture hat with ribbons. Under the picture hat were eyes hard and dark, though youthful; the chin was blue; there were freckles on the very Irish nose.

Despite the fact that this car was parked with lights out, these two were not embracing. They sat apart, the one behind the wheel staring straight ahead with infinite patience in his tired gray eyes, the other fidgeting and nervous.

On the knees of each rested a .38 caliber revolver.

The picture hat stirred impatiently, and from beneath it came a growly baritone. "I don't like jobs like this. What I like is murders."

Wentworth L. Morton said: "Shut up."

"This is small potatoes," complained the picture hat.

"So is most police work," said Morton, who ought to have known, having been, almost ever since anybody could remember, the best detective in the state. "Besides, don't be too sure we're not going to catch trouble anyway. The guy carries a gun, remember."

IN THE ORGANDY,

He fired twice into the carrion

disguised as a pick-up, was young McGarvey, recently
out of harness, the son of a cop who, until he was killed
at Morton's side in a gun battle some months before, had
been Morton's partner and best friend. Young McGarvey
was no intellectual wizard; but in a fight he was three men,

all dangerous. His thinking might have been elephantine, but his two hundred forty pounds could move with the speed of a cat. He was only a kid, only twenty-three.

"If this was anything but a small-timer," McGarvey growled, "he wouldn't be hanging around this one neighborhood. Three jobs, and all of them within a few hundred yards of each other."

"It is kind of funny about that. Funny the way the guy disappeared each time. The other night the radio boys chased him across the Otis estate, but they lost him somewhere in the shrubbery. They figured he must have got over to Poinsettia Drive—and yet nobody over there remembers hearing a car start up."

"Think it might be a servant on one of these estates?"

"I checked, and they all seem clear."

"Well, whoever he is, he's a small-timer. He's a punk."

"Listen, Sherlock," Morton said. "When a punk points a gun at you and pulls the trigger, it kills you just as dead as when a big-timer does the same thing."

They were silent for some time. Then McGarvey heard a car in Douglas Road, at the end of LaConcha, and he heard a radio. He turned his head.

"The patrol boys won't be coming this way, will they?"

"No. I fixed it that they shouldn't touch this road tonight."

"Thank God for that," McGarvey muttered. "I'd hate to have them see me in this rig!"

Morton never really laughed, he seldom even smiled, but now a tight grin cracked his face.

"Yes," he said, "I can believe that."

A few minutes later, as McGarvey was about to start some further complaint, Morton shushed him sharply.

"On the job, guy! Somebody's coming!"

"What do I have to do? I don't have to—"

"Get your head down on my shoulder here, you thick ox! Try to look as though you adored me."

"Geez! What a life!"

"You got to do a lot of things when you're a cop."

Three times in less than a week this prowler they sought had struck, each time at some point along little LaConcha Road, Coconut Grove. Each time the male half of a necking party had surrendered his valuables at the point of a pistol. There was no good description of the man. He wore a mask, and worked fast. If he had an automobile he hadn't brought it into LaConcha Road.

The car Morton had heard crept cautiously up LaConcha Road. It passed the Ford, and apparently its driver did not see that automobile. The driver appeared to be engrossed in a figure seated at his side: he had one arm around this figure.

McGarvey and Morton, though they said nothing, had the same thought at the same instant, which was: "Hell, here's a real necking party!" But they waited.

THE NEWCOMER'S CAR was a beauty, a long, glittering roadster. Only its cowl-lights and tail-light were aglow. It slid past the Ford, making scarcely a sound. Fifty or sixty yards further up the road it drew to the side. Its tail-light went out.

Morton, sighing, reached for the door.

"I'll go up and tell him to move along," he whispered.

"I'll tell him!"

"No, you stay here. The sight of a thing like you, looming up out of the darkness, might scare the guy to death."

Then, just when they were least expected, things began to happen.

A door of the roadster opened. A masked figure sprang out of the shrubbery, not six feet from that door. One stray moonbeam fell sparkling upon a revolver.

"Stick 'em up, brother, unless you want to—"

There were three shots. Somebody gasped, "Geez!" A figure in dinner clothes, in a large panama hat, toppled out of the roadster. The masked man turned, disappeared into the bushes. An engine bellowed, and the roadster shot away.

Morton had been half out of the Ford. There was no chance of stepping back in and starting the car in time to catch the roadster. So Morton kept going out. He knelt by the side of the road and fired two shots, deliberately, at the disappearing car. Then he vaulted a hedge and gave chase to the highwayman.

McGarvey? Poor McGarvey forgot that he was a female impersonator. He jumped out of the car, started to run toward the scene of the shooting, and, tripping on his skirt, fell heavily. He was up in an instant, roaring like a wounded bull. He grabbed the skirt in his left hand—his gun in the right—and instead of vaulting the hedge as Morton had done, he crashed right through it.

Two minutes later he found Morton. Miami's ace-detective looked unthrilled, unworried too. He was shaking his head.

"We could run around here all night and never get

anywhere. We'd only find ourselves popping at each other pretty soon."

McGarvey gasped: "Some guy took a slug back there!"

"I know. I saw him. That's one reason why I think we ought to go back. Look. You chase around for a while and see what you can see. But watch out that you don't plug anybody coming out of one of these houses around here."

Morton returned to LaConcha Road, while McGarvey, still holding his skirt high, plunged back and forth through foliage in pursuit of a phantom gunman.

McGarvey didn't find that gunman. It was, as Morton had pointed out, a hopeless task. The estates all ran together, with no walls or fences or thick hedges between them: it was like one enormous park. Very soon doors and windows were opening. People who had heard the shots were calling anxious questions. People were snapping on lights, and thoughtlessly standing in silhouette.

McGarvey returned to the road. Morton was gazing glumly at the body of a young man in dinner clothes.

"Smack in the heart," Morton said, "but no blood." He pointed to the dress shirt. "Funny about that, huh? No blood."

The radio patrol car appeared, screeching. Two uniformed cops tumbled out, each with a gun in his hand. One was tall and had lank yellow hair, like a Swede. He saw the body, and began to ask questions in an awed voice. The other cop was thick-set, dark. He saw McGarvey first— and started to laugh.

IT WAS A curious sound in that still and lovely place. The air was fragrant with the odor of roses, jasmine, bougain-villea. Florida moonlight struggled to get through the mango trees; coconut palms rattled apologetically. But in the midst of all this beauty was death—and a cop who couldn't stop laughing.

"*Hawf-hawf-hawf-hawf!* Whoops, dearie! Good old Garv putting on an act! *Hawf-hawf-hawf-hawf! U-uh-ugh!*"

McGarvey took a step toward the man.

"Shut up," he said, and his fists were doubled.

Morton said: "Shut up yourself. And take that hat off. Wouldn't you laugh, too?" To the blond cop he said: "Snap out of it, Anderson. Go up to Otis' house and get busy on a telephone. Wanted—the necker bandit. Wanted, also, a large dark roadster with the top up. Looks brand new. One man in it. Probably a couple of bullet-holes in the back. Tell 'em to flash that along the highway south. Homestead and Florida City and so forth."

A white-haired man came across the lawn. Behind him was a thin, sullen stripling in a double-breasted dinner suit.

"What is this?" the white-haired man demanded. He saw the uniforms. "Ah, the police! What's happened? Can I be of any help?"

Morton said: "Are you Mr. Otis?"

"Yes, I'm Mr. Otis. What's happened?"

"Then let this cop use your telephone, right away!"

"Why, of course. My nephew will show him where it is. Guy, take this officer to the house and show him the telephone."

But Guy Otis had seen the corpse.

"Why, I knew that man!" he cried. "That's Harry Shall-cross! I ran into him only last night, at the Everleigh."

Otis gave his nephew a hard look. Guy Otis added hastily that he hadn't been playing at the Everleigh—only dropped in to look at the place.

"Well, never mind that now," Otis said. "Take this officer inside and show him the telephone." He looked sadly at the body. "Killed right in front of my house," he muttered. "Practically on my property."

"Right before our eyes," McGarvey said bitterly.

But Morton shook his head. "Take a better look at that body, Garv."

McGarvey glanced curiously at his partner; but he knelt beside the body, touched the face. He started back.

"It's *cold!*"

"Yeah," said Morton. "Look at how stiff it is, too. Look at the way those hands are clawed."

"But we saw him killed right here, and it takes hours for—"

"Sure. The necker bandit shot him through the heart, but that wasn't what killed him. There's a bullet hole just above the right ear. No blood on the shirt-front, but there's blood on the side of the head."

Morton, talking only for young McGarvey's benefit, had the air of a pedagogue. He all but waggled a forefinger as he explained.

"The body was stiff when he fell out of the car. I saw that. Another thing. There were two different guns fired. The bandit shot once, with what was a thirty-two, or maybe a thirty-eight. The guy in the roadster shot twice, and his gun was smaller, probably a twenty-two. You could tell by the sound. That guy either had his gun out, and was all set for trouble, or else he's mighty quick on the draw. That's why I fired. I couldn't be sure, then, but I had an idea we'd want to know more about that car. So I fired low, hoping to mark it. The necker bandit, like you said, Garv, is a small-timer. All he murdered was a corpse. But the other baby! That's different."

The dark-haired cop still was laughing. He leaned against a tree, and laughed so hard that tears rolled down his cheeks.

2

GAMBLER'S PALACE

THEY GOT TO the Everleigh a little after two. It was a big place, built in the days of the boom. The depression had rendered it extremely sick. For two seasons it had staggered along, losing money. Then for several seasons it was closed. It had opened one winter as a noisy nightclub, trading on its past glories. Then it had been closed again.

The Everleigh represented a staggering investment, and the fact that it was now being reopened, and was to be grander than ever, had set Miamians crowing about the return of good times.

The Ford in which Morton and McGarvey arrived— McGarvey was in normal attire now—seemed dwarfed by the magnificence of an entrance designed for nothing less than Cunninghams and Daimlers.

"They shouldn't allow gambling in this town," McGarvey grumbled. "All it does is make trouble. Anyway, it isn't right."

"Vannest is a nice guy," Morton said carelessly.

"I don't like any gamblers," said McGarvey.

After a doorkeeper had been made to believe that these shabby ruffians were detectives, George Vannest himself appeared. He was a man of forty-five or fifty, but slim and straight, youthful of figure, with a springy step. His hair was dead white. His face was tanned; his eyes were a dark, direct blue, with pleasant little wrinkles at the outside corners. He never had been known to raise his voice. He wore full evening clothes which his own best customer might have envied.

"My old pal, Morton! Swell to see you again! Swell!"

McGarvey frowned in disapproval. Morton nodded, blinking; he shook Vannest's hand.

"This is young McGarvey. You remember Garv? This is his son."

Why, of course Vannest remembered McGarvey! A fine cop if there ever was one! If the son was half as good as his father, God help the crooks in Miami, eh?

Young McGarvey, being Irish, enjoyed flattery; but he was cop enough to be suspicious, and kid enough to feel embarrassed.

"Yeah," he growled.

"Come to look over the new plant?" Vannest asked them. "Swell! Let me take you around myself, eh?"

"We came here on business," McGarvey said significantly.

Morton said: "Well, let's see the place first, anyway. I been meaning to get out here." His solemn eyes were taking in an entrance hall which would have awed an emperor. "The big fellas must have sunk a lot of dough into this shack, George."

"That they did, Mort! They certainly did! All new furnishings, new equipment, new gardens. Suppose we start by looking around outside, eh?"

Well, there was everything. There were clipped hedges,

ornamental borders, jets and ripples of water, and still
pools packed with lilies; Pavonazetto marble columns,
garden statues, Roman benches; there were terraces, tables
in unexpected places, expressionless waiters; there were
loggias designed after those in the Pisani palace at Venice;
there was a very Seventeenth Century garden bathed in
moonlight which every Miamian knows to be superior to
the moonlight of Italy.

The main building itself, constructed of travertine and
Cuban coral, had a roof of weathered antique tiles. It had
been modeled upon sundry celebrated palaces; and the
result, though a trifle confusing, was breathtaking too.
Inside were Carrara marble fireplaces, grillwork doorways
from the shops of masters, Aubusson and Hispano-Maur-
esque rugs, Ferrarese tapestries. Somewhat more modern
were the two bars, the intimate café, the ballroom where a
world-famous orchestra played, the big reception cham-
bers, the stag grill, the three large gambling salons.

"Certainly is the cat's," conceded young McGarvey.

Only one of the gambling salons was open. Too early in
the season, yet, to open the others. The place was moderately crowded.

"Drink?" asked Vannest.

"Thanks," said Morton, who also accepted a cigar.

"You, McGarvey?"

McGarvey said: "I don't drink."

When Morton had finished his highball he looked
around once more, nodding thoughtfully, admiringly. Then
he said to Vannest: "About this business—"

"Oh, yes."

"There was a murder committed."

"Dear, dear! Shall we go to my office?"

IT WAS A severely rich place, compact, comfortable, extremely quiet. There was a large, bank-presidenty desk, with a high-backed chair behind it. Vannest didn't sit in that chair: he sat on the edge of the desk.

He said: "Young Shallcross, eh? Yes, of course I know him. He was in here last night. Right in this room, if it comes to that."

"What was he doing here?"

"He'd lost. Not much. About three hundred. And he came in here to make out a check. I didn't step in with him. I came in a few minutes afterward—because he knew where the blank checkbook was, and I happened to be busy about something."

"You deposited that check yet?"

"He tore it up. Decided at the last minute to pay me cash."

Morton asked: "Why?"

"Well, he had about five or six hundred. I'm guessing, you understand, but it was about that much. And he'd decided to go night-clubbing. He's likely to throw money away when he gets tight, so he figured the less he had the better."

"What time did he go?"

"About eleven. He used this side door here. It leads directly down to the side entrance."

"Why'd he go that way?"

Vannest shrugged. "His car was nearer the side entrance, than the front entrance, I suppose."

"How was he dressed, remember?"

"Well, he had on dinner clothes. And that big panama

he always wears. He wears it even inside here. Won't check it. Just an eccentricity, I suppose. And I seem to recall that last night he wore a white waistcoat and a bat-wing tie."

Morton leaned back in a squashy, soothing chair.

"It's a funny thing," Morton said. "He was dressed like that when we found him tonight, but he had about two hundred bucks in his pockets."

"Looks as though he didn't go out drinking after all then, doesn't it?"

"Yes—another thing, the doc says he was probably dead about twenty-four hours. If that's right, and if you're right about the time, then he must have caught the slug within a few hours of when he left here."

"Seems so, doesn't it? I'm sure about that time. I remember because I had a big party coming a little after eleven, and I was getting things set for them. That was why I didn't come directly into the office here with Shallcross."

Morton nodded, rose. He strolled over to the smaller door, by which Vannest said Shallcross had quit the office. He opened this door and peered down well lighted steps.

"Many of the guests use this?"

"It depends. A few do, who know about it, if they happen to have left their cars around near there. We keep a sort of doorman there, in a pillbox just outside. I don't know whether he was on duty when Shallcross went out, but if he wasn't he should have been."

"We'll ask him," Morton decided.

THE DOORMAN WAS a tall youngster with a goodnatured grin. Yes, he remembered Mr. Shallcross coming out last night. It was along around eleven o'clock. He asked if he should bring up Mr. Shallcross' car, but Mr. Shallcross had merely waved him aside.

"He usually speaks, but he seemed kind of thoughtful last night."

"What do you mean, thoughtful?"

"Well, he was walking along with his head down. He waved to me—sort of saluted me—but he didn't say anything."

Morton yawned, threw away a cigar butt, looked at McGarvey.

"Well, what do you say, Sherlock? Shall we call it a night?"

George Vannest walked with them to the blue Ford. He shook hands with both of them. He said he hoped they cleared the case up promptly and to their satisfaction. He was sure they would.

"I like that guy, even if he is a gambler," McGarvey announced, as they drove away between rows of royal palms, "but still and all, there's something phony about him somewhere."

"George has a nice job there," said Morton.

They went to the garage of the hotel at which Harry Shallcross had been staying. The night attendant remembered seeing Mr. Shallcross come in the previous evening, a little after eleven. Mr. Shallcross had driven into an empty space, got out, walked away.

"He usually leaves the car right in the middle of the floor here, and lets me put it away, but last night he seemed to be in a hurry. He just waved to me and walked out, with his head down."

Morton asked: "You remember how he was dressed?"

"Like he usually is, nights. Had on a tuxedo, and that big panama. I never was very close to him. I was up the other end there, putting a car away."

They went to the morgue. There was to be an autopsy first thing in the morning, and Morton wished to examine the body again before it was undressed. He was particularly interested in the bat-wing tie, which was none too neatly knotted.

Young McGarvey stared at him, wondering. Nobody ever knew what Morton was thinking, not even young McGarvey.

McGarvey asked, at last: "Got any ideas?"

"Yeah," said Morton, sighing. "I got an idea it's time for us to go to bed."

SERGEANT WENTWORTH L. MORTON was a quiet, logical, direct sort of man, stolid, steady, slow-moving, and apparently without imagination. But he saw things other men didn't see. He got things done. And in fact, though nobody ever had seen him hurry, he worked more than any other man in the department. Work was a habit with him—an unconscious habit, like smoking.

The morning after the finding of Harry Shallcross' body, Morton was at headquarters exceptionally early. He had cleared his desk when a report came in that the roadster had been found abandoned in a small side road near Florida City. A 1935 Cadillac, except for two bullet holes in the back just above the gas tank, it was in perfect condition. According to its speedometer, it had been driven only 3,442 miles.

Morton jotted down the license number, the engine number. Then he put in a call for Tallahassee.

He was sending telegrams when Captain Montgomery appeared.

"Figured out yet who killed that Shallcross kid?"

"Yeah, but I'm likely wrong. Still a lot to do."

"How many men do you want?"

Morton said, without looking up: "Garv's enough."

"If you ask me," said Montgomery, "young Garv's a tough baby and all like that, but he's not quite bright."

"No. But he's handy to have around in case of trouble."

"You're not expecting trouble, are you?"

"I always expect trouble," said Morton.

Soon afterward a report came in from the fingerprint-men who had gone over the roadster carefully with their powder and their little camel's-hair brushes—and had found nothing whatever.

Young McGarvey, fresh from breakfast, took this report by telephone. He hung up in disgust.

"Well, *that* don't tell us anything!"

"It tells us a lot, maybe," said Morton.

McGarvey cried: "You got something in your bean, and you're working on it. I wish to hell you'd let me know what it is!"

"I like to be sure about things first," said Morton.

When the autopsy report came in, it didn't satisfy him. He telephoned one of physicians.

"Well, yes. It did look as though somebody had been probing for the bullet. I figured you cops had done it, last night."

Morton grunted a rebuke.

"Don't they usually arch their backs when they stiffen up?"

"Well, that depends a good deal on the position."

"Then this guy might have been sitting down when *rigor mortis* set in?"

"Might have been, yes. In fact, he probably was."

"I see," said Morton. "Thanks."

HE WORKED IN silence, methodically, for several hours, while McGarvey glowered. McGarvey considered his partner, his father's friend, the greatest man in the world; but sometimes he wished that Morton wouldn't treat him like a school boy.

Then Morton sent for Cassidy.

Cassidy was a detective Miami had "borrowed" for the season from the City of New York. He was supposed to be "studying conditions" in the Florida resort.

"A guy named Chester A. Marshall, age forty-two, five feet nine, blue eyes, brown hair, gives his address as Five Hundred, Broadway—if that means anything. And with him is a guy named Joey or Joe something, about the same age, dark hair, dark eyes, a little bigger." Morton shuffled telegrams and papers. "That Caddy roadster was registered in Marshall's name, only four days ago, at Jacksonville. Filed a bill of sale from North Carolina." He shuffled some more papers. "Before that he had it registered in Baltimore, and before that in Philly, and before that in New York. That's where he bought the car, in New York. Bought it brand new, and paid cash. Catch on?"

Cassidy thought for a minute.

"Might be Chesty Mears and Joey Horowitz. I know they're in town because I saw them day before yesterday. They're at the Everglades, under their right names. They both got records, but nothing big. A couple of cheap chiselers. Used to make a book, in New York. Haven't heard what they've been doing lately. I stopped them the other day and asked them questions, but I didn't pick them up because they seemed to be behaving themselves all right."

"Would they be likely to work a game like this?"

"They might."

"Are they driving a Caddy roadster?"

"I wouldn't know. Find out for you?"

"I'll go over with you," said Morton.

McGarvey blurted: "What's all this about, anyway?"

Morton took his arm, led him outside. Morton explained, as they started for the Hotel Everglades, the nature of the racket.

"A guy buys a swell new sporty-looking car, and gets a *bona fide* title, and he takes it out on the road and sells it over and over again. The trick feature about it is that his sucker-list is a list of smart guys in each town. Gamblers, politicians, nightclub proprietors—guys who like to make a show, and who think they know a lot.

"Well, this guy goes to one of them and tells him here's a car he can have cheap as dirt. It's a two-thousand-dollar job, say, and he offers it for three or four hundred—provided it's cash on the table and no questions asked. The sucker naturally figures it's a hot car. He figures he's taking some chances in buying it, but that if he gets in any real trouble, and gets picked up, he can beat a possession-of-stolen-goods rap because of his pull. So he buys the car. And the man who really owns it, pockets the dough and fades. The sucker thinks he'll never see that man again.

"But the guy keeps a duplicate key. In fact, he keeps a lot of them. He stays in the town until he gets a chance to steal the car. When the theft is discovered, the sucker, thinking it was a hot car, doesn't dare report it. But even if he did report it, and even if they pick up the guy in the car, what have they got on him? He simply denies the sale, which of course wasn't legitimate in the first place. And all the time he's got an authentic title to the car. It's his, and he can prove it. What are they going to do? Nothing. So he drives it to the next town, and sells it to another smart aleck who thinks he's getting a hot job cheap, and he steals it again and drives it away again. He can keep that up indefinitely."

"Unless one of the suckers happens to catch up with him and makes it a personal affair," Cassidy amended.

McGarvey said: "I think I get it—you mean, these guys Marshall and Joey whatever-his-name-is were selling that Caddy all the way down here from New York, and they still got it?"

"Looks like it. With the car registered in five different states, within two months, and yet it's been driven only a little over three thousand miles."

MR. MEARS AND Mr. Horowitz weren't in, hadn't been seen around the Everglades since the previous afternoon; but the house dick, a friend of Morton, took the detectives upstairs and used a passkey.

Mr. Mears and Mr. Horowitz had not slept in their beds. They were traveling light—only two suitcases—but they obligingly left records. There was a Florida State title to the Cadillac roadster. Even more important, there was a little black notebook.

"The sucker list," reported Cassidy. "Business was good. Here's Miami. It says—'Vannest, Walsh, Aveson, Steinberg.' Then opposite the first name it says—'Fell fast, two C's.' Who are these guys?"

"They're all big gamblers around here," McGarvey cried, "and it looks as though George Vannest had been taken in."

Morton said slowly: "It does look that way, doesn't it?" He took the book, studied it. "There's something else it says under the last name here. 'Collect for M. Scholtz. Promised fifty split.' We got no M. Scholtz around here that I know of."

"Horowitz and Mears used to work for a gambler named Maxie Scholtz, in New York," Cassidy offered. "Maxie's in the big dough, now. Runs a joint on Park Avenue. But he's one wise worker, Maxie is. If you're thinking of asking the boys in New York to get something out of him, save yourself the trouble."

"What we ought to do," cried McGarvey, "is pick up George Vannest! If these two chiselers sold him that car, then he must have been the man who dumped out Shallcross' body last night!"

"There's no hurry," Morton said thoughtfully. "George isn't going to run away. And as far as getting him to talk is concerned, George is just about in a class with this Scholtz guy Cassidy tells us about."

He turned to the house detective. "Will you watch for these men, Mac, and pick them up the minute you see them? Bring 'em over to headquarters. I'll be there. I think," he told nobody in particular, "that when we get this guy Mears and this guy Horowitz, we'll have the answers to a lot of hard questions."

Then Morton went back to his office, back to work. Newspaper readers, made familiar with Morton's exploits, probably thought of him as a tall, romantic personage, a human bloodhound. In fact, he looked less like a detective than a commission merchant, or a serious-minded banker. He refused to run around, to talk in a loud voice. He never made an arrest until he was sure of himself. His persistence, his quiet toil, were tantalizing. Even Captain Montgomery, who knew him well, was troubled. There ought, somehow, to be more noise and fuss connected with a murder investigation. And young McGarvey, who had nothing to do but sit and fret, was furious.

"We ought to pick up this guy, Vannest," McGarvey said again and again. "He's a nice guy, but he's a gambler, and I never trust gamblers. They oughtn't to allow it here anyway."

Morton said: "You couldn't get anything out of George Vannest with dynamite."

"But he certainly bought that car!"

"I wonder—George is a pretty wise guy. Too wise to be tumbling for an old racket like that."

Twice that afternoon the house detective at the Everglades telephoned to report that there had been no sign of Mears and Horowitz. At about four o'clock young Guy Otis called.

"Since I talked to you last night," Guy Otis said, "I've remembered that I saw Harry Shallcross after I left the Everleigh the other night. I'd forgotten about it. I saw him on Biscayne Boulevard, near the Everglades Hotel. I think he was just about to go into the hotel, but I can't be sure of that."

Morton asked: "What time was this?"

"Oh, maybe a quarter of twelve, or twelve o'clock. Harry was alone, and on foot."

"You going to be home for a little while? I was thinking of driving over to your place for another look around the grounds. Maybe you could tell me more about it personally?"

"Well, I don't think there's anything else to tell, except that I did see Harry Shallcross in front of the Everglades. But of course I'd be glad to see you if you want to come here. Yes, I'll be around. My uncle's here, too."

3

BUZZARDS AND BODIES

IT WAS A relief for young McGarvey, who drove too fast. It gave him something to do besides sit in the office and try to guess what his sidekick was thinking.

Guy Otis was friendly, but he had nothing to add to his story.

"Can't imagine why I forgot to tell you this last night. I guess it must have been the excitement."

Morton didn't appear to be much interested. He asked some perfunctory questions. Edward T. Otis was there, obviously not pleased to be reminded that his nephew had been at the Everleigh. He seemed to share McGarvey's opinion of gamblers and gambling.

Morton asked suddenly: "Could I use your telephone?"

"Of course! Of course!"

Morton called George Vannest. He was in the hall, but his voice carried clearly to the three men in the library.

"Will you be in tonight at about ten, George?... Yeah, a little more checking up.... I can't ask you now, because I got to get some more dope first, but I'd like to know that I'll be able to reach you at ten tonight... You will? Fine. You'll be in your office, eh? All right. Be there alone, won't you?... Thanks."

When Morton returned to the library, McGarvey said darkly: "There's the man who committed this murder, George Vannest."

Otis asked: "What makes you think so?"

"Because he was the driver of that car," McGarvey explained. "What he did was shoot Shallcross right in his office there, which I happen to know is soundproof. And then he put on Shallcross' hat and his coat and his bat-wing tie, and he walked out, nodding to the doorman but not speaking. He got into Shallcross' car, using the keys he'd taken from the body, and drove to the garage and left the car. He was careful to keep his head down. He's an older man than Shallcross, but about the same build, and under that big panama, and in a tuxedo, he was able to pass for Shallcross. That was to establish that Shallcross had left the Everleigh, see? As a matter of fact, Vannest didn't know what to do with the body at first, and he waited until last night to ditch it. He picked out LaConcha Road because he figured that would make it look like the necker bandit's work."

Morton asked: "When did you dope all this out, Garv?"

"I'm not as dumb as I look! Shallcross was probably in a sitting position when he was killed, and for some time after that. Otherwise he wouldn't have stiffened up the way he did, arching in instead of back. And didn't you notice when we talked to Vannest early this morning that he was careful not to sit in that big chair behind the desk? Why? Because even Vannest has some feeling about things, and he couldn't forget that he'd had a corpse in that chair for quite a while." He turned to Morton. "Isn't that what you've been figuring?"

"Yes, as a matter of fact, it is."

"And another thing. Harry Shallcross' necktie wasn't tied very neat. Why? Because Vannest had taken it off, and worn it himself to establish the departure, and then he'd tied it back on Shallcross again. It's pretty hard to tie a bow tie on somebody else. Everything about Shallcross was neat as a pin—except that necktie."

Otis asked: "Well then, why don't you arrest Vannest?"

"That's what I want to know," said McGarvey.

"I'll tell you a secret," Morton confided. "I am going to arrest him. Late tonight, or else tomorrow morning. I want to clear up a few little things first, before I crack a confession out of him."

NOW HE LOOKED not at all like a tired bishop. His gray-blue eyes were cold, his gray brows were low, his jaw was set. McGarvey stared at him in astonishment.

"I thought you said that nobody could make Vannest talk?"

Morton said, savagely: "I'll make that mug talk, don't worry!" He appealed to the Otises. "Of course you gentlemen understand that this is strictly confidential. McGarvey and I really shouldn't be talking like this in front of you."

"Of course," cried Edward T. Otis; and Guy Otis echoed him.

"And now what I'd like to do is have another good look around the grounds." Morton turned to Guy Otis. "Want to show me around?"

McGarvey said: "I'm going down toward Florida City. Going to have a look at that place where the car was found."

Morton only shrugged. McGarvey got funny notions sometimes.

Still, Morton's example was having its effect Young McGarvey was noticing things. For instance, he noticed the buzzards on the way to the place where the car had been found. This was not far from the edge of the Everglades, where buzzards wheel pauselessly overhead—big, awkward, rust-colored, slow-moving beasts untiring in their search for dead or dying animals. But it was unusual to see them so far east. Ten or twelve of them circled above a hummock, a thick island of undergrowth in the midst of a flat wilderness. Now and then, one would drop into that undergrowth. It was near the highway. In fact, two of the birds were on the edge of the pavement—grotesque figures of decay, with hunched shoulders, with long skinny necks and bright, beady, red eyes. Blood was slobbered over their beaks.

McGarvey turned the wheel sharply, and slapped the horn button with the heel of his right hand.

"Out of my way, ye filthy carrion!"

They spread monstrous wings and flapped heavily off.

Yes, it was curious to see buzzards so far from the 'Glades. McGarvey watched them in his mirror, noticed that more were coming constantly. There was a strong breeze from the direction of the sea, and no doubt this had carried the scent.

"Probably some poor mutt crawled in there to die," McGarvey growled to himself.

He had no difficulty locating the little sideroad where the Cadillac had been abandoned. He got out and examined the ground thoroughly. And again he found something.

He was getting excited now. He was beginning to think he was a pretty good detective after all.

What he found was half a pearl cufflink.

"Somebody had on a dress suit," he told himself.

He wondered what Morton would say about this. He still was wondering about Morton when he started back.

McGarvey didn't think readily. It was an effort, and it absorbed him. But this day it didn't absorb him to such an extent that he failed to notice the buzzards again.

There were many more of them now, at least thirty. They concentrated on that hummock. McGarvey passed them, but he watched them in his mirror. Thirty buzzards for one dead rabbit, or one dead dog? He got curious about this. He stopped, turned back.

When he climbed out of the car he had an uneasy sense of horror. His chest felt tight, and his stomach wavered. He couldn't explain this.

THE BIRDS, TANTALIZINGLY, waited until he was almost upon them before they rose into the air. They moved cumbrously. One, succumbing to panic, flew straight for McGarvey's face. Its blood-stained beak brushed his chin, its foul feathers slapped his forehead. He cursed, drew his pistol, shot the bird. It fluttered for a short distance, and then fell; and instantly five or six of its fellows were upon it—for a buzzard isn't fussy about food.

McGarvey, swearing furiously, was excited, and a little frightened. He fired twice into the carrion crowded around the bird he had wounded. They rose into the air; but soon they descended upon their victim again.

The hummock was silent. The smell was frightful as McGarvey pushed his way through tropical weeds and parasites.

When he saw what the buzzards had been eating it

made him instantly, violently sick, and he ran away from the hummock. It was some time before he was able to wipe off his mouth, wipe his forehead, plunge into the bushes again. The buzzards wheeled in lumbrous circles overhead, waiting for a chance to resume the feast too long denied them.

Half an hour later, when McGarvey reached the nearest telephone, and called the Otis residence, his hand still trembled, his face still was wet with sweat and pale.

He told Morton: "You can call off that house dick at the Everglades. Mears and Horowitz aren't coming back."

Morton, when he arrived, studied the two hideous things with no more apparent emotion than a bridge player might show in studying a freshly dealt hand. What interested him most was the fact that there had been no attempt to remove marks of identification. Laundry tabs, belt initials, were there; and there were papers and letters in the pockets of both men. Horowitz had been shot once, between the eyes. Mears had been shot five times in the chest and stomach. The buzzards hadn't left enough of either face for identification by photograph, nor enough of the four hands to get fingerprints, but the bodies hadn't been searched. There was a wrist watch on what remained of Mears' right wrist, and Horowitz had been gripping a big old-fashioned Spanish revolver.

"I'd say Vannest!" McGarvey cried. "These punks put one over on him, and he got sore and shot them up!"

But Morton shook his head.

"George is smooth. He wouldn't pull a job like this. Whoever shot these boys must have emptied a whole gun at them. He must have lost his head. Besides, why this museum piece?" He picked up the Spanish revolver. It was not loaded. He sniffed the muzzle. "Hasn't been fired. As a matter of fact, I don't think the thing will shoot! The hammer's busted."

"I'd say arrest Vannest!"

Morton stared sadly at his partner.

"Listen, Garv. Don't you be going nuts and picking up George Vannest! He's smart stuff, George is. He's no punk to be pushed around like some street-corner sport you don't like."

"I thought you were talking about pushing him around yourself."

"Yeah, I was *talking* about it," said Morton; and thereafter he refused to discuss the case.

It irritated young McGarvey, who glowered, sulked. If Morton had been less absorbed in his work he would have noticed this, would have corrected it by taking McGarvey into his confidence. It was not that he didn't trust McGarvey, or didn't like him. But he simply couldn't seem to take the kid seriously. And now, wrapped up in his job, he had all the detachment of a chess champion. He forgot everything but the problem upon which he was working.

McGARVEY FORGOT A few things, too. For instance, he forgot about the cuff-link; and when he did remember it he didn't tell Morton, or anybody else. He'd do some work himself! If Morton was going to work alone—which was what it amounted to—then young McGarvey could work alone too. He'd show them he was something more than a husky dumbbell!

Morton didn't even notice him. Morton was sending wires, receiving wires, making long-distance calls, studying reports. At nine o'clock that evening he looked around for McGarvey and couldn't find him. He shrugged, went outside. The car they used, which McGarvey usually drove, was there; and the keys were in the ignition; but there was no sign of McGarvey. Morton went to a restaurant and slowly, silently, ate an enormous steak. Then he got into the department car and drove to the Everleigh. It was twenty minutes to ten.

George Vannest, as always, was affable.

"Thought you were going to give me a ring at ten!"

"I decided to come and see you, instead."

"Fine! Just step into the office, won't you, Mort? I'll be tied up for a few minutes."

Morton utilized the time. He locked the office door from the inside, and went to work. He searched the drawers; he examined the blotters, the wastebasket, a checkbook; he looked long and hard at the big desk chair.

In one drawer he found a box of .22 cartridges, but he didn't find a pistol.

He was backing away from the desk, wondering about this, when the shots were fired.

There were three shots in rapid succession. Morton, not unaccustomed to the sound of bullets, knew even as he dropped to the floor how breathlessly close death had come. One of the bullets literally had fanned his cheek. He didn't like that.

Now there was silence, except for the sound of an orchestra on the south terrace. Outside George Vannest's office window, as Morton could see from the floor, a big Florida moon sailed serenely over the tops of coco palms.

The terrace music ceased, and Morton could hear the rustle of hibiscus bushes, the gentle *lap-lap* of wavelets.

On hands and knees he went to the side door. He let himself out, raced downstairs. His hand was on his gun.

The good natured young doorman looked alarmed. Shots? No, he hadn't heard any shots. He'd been shifting a couple of cars, and maybe that was why. Was Sergeant Morton certain of this? Wouldn't it be wise to report the matter to Mr. Vannest?

"Forget it," Morton said. "I was probably mistaken. Yes. It was probably backfires."

Morton was staring at the shrubbery near the edge of the bay—the shrubbery from which he was certain the shots had been fired. But he didn't go in that direction. He was no coward, but he was no fool either. He went back to Vannest's office. He examined the bullet holes. They were not conspicuous in the dark walnut paneling, but the slugs had penetrated too far for him to be able to pry them out.

He unlocked the door, and when George Vannest entered, a few minutes later, he was seated at one end of the desk.

He asked some stale questions. He didn't mention the shooting. Vannest was polite, but obviously puzzled.

"Getting anywhere with this case, Mort? It's none of my business, of course, but you seem to be just going over the same territory again and again."

"It's a tough case," Morton admitted. "Well, I'll be going."

MORTON'S THINKING WAS completed now, and he became really conscious of his partner's absence. He was annoyed. The time for action had arrived, and where was

McGarvey? It was a comforting thing to have young
McGarvey at your side when things got rough. Besides,
Morton didn't like to drive.

He phoned headquarters from a booth, but McGarvey wasn't there. He made another call from that booth.
Then he drove slowly and seriously to Douglas Road, near
LaConcha. He parked the car, snapped off the lights, and
struck out across the dark expanse of the Evans estate.

He moved very carefully, avoiding open patches of
moonlight. Just before he entered the Otis estate he drew
and cocked his gun.

He was wishing McGarvey was with him. McGarvey
liked the rough stuff; but he, Morton, was getting a bit
old for it.

But there wasn't time to go looking for McGarvey. A
killer was loose, was about to strike again.

An amateur killer, too. One who had lost his head. Irre-
sponsible and unaccountable, for all practical purposes a
madman.

Morton moved with extraordinary care. He encircled the
Otis residence, encircled every cleared space, and moved
through bushes like an impalpable wraith. He kept his gun
raised and ready.

It took him twenty minutes to reach that part of LaConcha Road which was shadowed by the mango trees and the
edge of the Otis estate.

There he paused, upright and alert, beside a protective
clump of palmettos. The shrubbery at this point was especially thick, and Morton, after all, was no primitive American Indian with the instincts of a jungle beast. Prowling

like this, it was conceivable that he might literally collide with the man he sought.

For that man was near. Morton was sure of it. And sooner or later, that man, lacking Morton's patience, would move restlessly.

So Morton waited.

Earlier in the evening there had been crowds here, souvenir hunters, motorists curious to gaze upon the place where a body had been found. But now LaConcha Road was deserted. An automobile hummed along Douglas Road, out of sight. Far behind Morton somewhere came the blat of a radio. Otherwise there was no sound. Most of the houses were utterly dark.

Morton had laid his plans carefully; he thought he knew just what to expect; and with that wonderful patience of his, he might have waited hours without stirring. But even Morton's plans could be ruined. An automobile came up LaConcha Road.

4

FLAMING GUNS

IT CAME VERY slowly and quietly, with lights out. In the darkness, Morton frowned. He tried to see who was in the car. He prayed that it wouldn't stop here.

But it did stop. It stopped not fifteen feet from where he was standing. The door opened.

Morton yelled: "George! *Duck!*"

There was a spatter of gunfire on his right. Three or four shots. He swung in that direction, saw the flashes, fired. He dropped to one knee, and fired again.

Then there were two cracks from the road. Morton's right hand went furiously hot, and he realized that he wasn't holding his gun any more. He threw himself upon his face, fumbling on the ground with his left hand.

There was another shot from the bushes.

Morton still was scrabbling for his gun. He heard a familiar shout, rolled over on his side, saw young McGarvey charging up LaConcha Road.

McGarvey was so excited that he'd forgotten to draw his own pistol. The big Irish fool was racing into danger with only two swinging fists for weapons.

"*Down, Garv!*"

But McGarvey wasn't a fast thinker. He saw George

Vannest with a gun in his hand. Vannest saw him, might have killed him, hesitated.

"Down, you ape!"

Two more explosions. The man in the bushes was firing at the sound of Morton's voice.

But this time McGarvey also recognized that voice; and he realized that his partner was in trouble. He whirled on his right heel, swung his right arm out, and slapped Vannest's mouth with such a terrific backhand blow that the gambler was knocked down upon the running board of his own car.

Then McGarvey went charging for the bushes. You never could teach McGarvey anything about ordinary caution.

Still, you can't beat dumb luck. Young Guy Otis stepped out of the bushes, deliberately raised his pistol, leveled it at the onrushing detective. He pulled the trigger—and got a click!

McGarvey started hitting him. Very soon McGarvey was sitting on him, still hitting him.

"Lay off, ox!" Morton was on his feet now. His right hand and right wrist hurt like hell, but he walked over to McGarvey. "You want to kill that kid?"

"Well, he tried to kill you, didn't he?"

"Stop it! What the hell are you doing here, anyway?"

"If it comes to that," retorted McGarvey, "what the hell are you doing here?"

George Vannest, sitting up on his running board, called bitterly: "Of all the crazy cops I ever saw—"

"Who's crazy?"

McGarvey rose from a now motionless Guy Otis, and

moved toward George Vannest. When McGarvey started hitting people he hated to stop. Morton, with his left hand, grabbed his partner's coat collar.

"Will you shut up and stop trying to smack everybody in sight? Take that kid to his uncle's house and call a doctor. And thank your crazy luck that he was fool enough to shoot his gun out before you arrived." To Vannest he called: "Come on, George. As soon as we get to where I can have a drink, I want you to tell me what *you're* doing here, too!"

"I—I'm sorry about that wrist, Mort. I didn't know it was you, then. I just shot at the flash."

"All right, all right! Come on!"

McGARVEY, WHEN THINGS had quieted, when Guy Otis had been taken away, was apologetic.

"I got sore," he admitted, "and I set out to crack the case myself. I was dead certain I was right about Vannest, here, killing Shallcross and then trying to make it look as though Shallcross had left the place alive. And when I found this thing"—he produced the half cuff-link—"then I was more certain than ever. It looked like the thing a man would wear with full soup-and-fish, instead of just a tux. I figured that when Vannest found he'd lost it he'd throw the other link away—most likely he'd throw away the whole set, studs and links and all."

Morton, mollified, bandaged, and with a highball in his left hand, turned to George Vannest.

"See? The kid isn't quite as dumb as he looks. But of course, Garv, you should have told me about that."

"I know. I'm sorry. But I was sore, and I decided to have a look through Vannest's apartment. It was a risky thing to do, I suppose, without a warrant or anything—but I did it. I didn't take the police car because I didn't want to be seen driving up to the apartment house in it. So I took my own car. I got into the apartment with an ordinary skeleton key. I—I guess I kind of mussed things up in there."

"Don't mention it," said Vannest, not talking clearly because of the condition of his mouth. "And what did you find?"

"Two jewelers' boxes with studs and links, and two without. You'd be wearing one set, but what about the other? Besides, this half link exactly fits into one of the spaces." He nodded to Vannest. "So, you talk about me being thick, huh?"

"You're absolutely right," Vannest said. "I should have thrown box and all away. Can't imagine why I didn't."

"Well, then I was determined to arrest you. I phoned Mort, but he wasn't at headquarters, so I went to the Everleigh alone. You were just driving out as I started in, so I decided to trail you. Well, so you came to LaConcha Road." He appealed to Morton. "Now will you tell me what it's all about?"

Morton finished his drink. He looked at Vannest.

"First of all, I want to know why you came here."

The gambler shrugged.

"I got scared. It's no fun having a dick like you just in back, Mort. Tonight you had me guessing. You meant to ask me something important, when you first came to the club, but all you did ask were routine questions—stuff you'd asked before. So I figured you must have found something in the office which had made you change your mind. I knew it wouldn't do any good to ask you. You never do tell anybody anything."

McGarvey cried: "Ain't that the truth though?"

"So I started snooping around, to see if you'd spotted something I'd missed. And I found those bullet holes. I reasoned that if that had happened while you were there, you'd go out by that side door and ask the doorman if he'd heard anything. So I went there and asked him, and it turns out that's exactly what you did do. Then I figured that young Otis had gone completely off his nut, and he was out gunning for me. So I went after him. I didn't intend to kill him. All I meant to do was park here quietly, get hold of him, show him my own gun, and throw the fear of God into his heart. But when I stopped, and started to get out of the car, he began to pop at me from the bushes. How could he have known I was coming?"

Morton said: "Because I told him."

"*You* told him! But I didn't know myself until just—"

McGarvey cried: "What about starting this thing at the beginning? You've both got me balled up now."

MORTON LOOKED SADLY at his empty glass. He sighed. "Well, I'd figured Guy Otis as the necker bandit almost from the start. He was a fool for gambling, and his uncle wouldn't give him any more money. He knew this territory thoroughly, particularly this estate. He might have noticed the necking parties some time when he was out walking and trying to think of how to get money. He probably figured he'd be the very last person in the world anybody would suspect. Also, he could get away easily, and he could ditch his gun easily.

"The gun was what I needed. If I could catch him with

that, then I'd have a case against him, since a bullet fired from it would match up with the slug we took out of Harry Shallcross' heart. But how could I find the gun? The kid certainly wouldn't be so foolish as to hide it in his room. Anyway, if I got a search warrant—assuming I *could* get one—it would tip him off. I figured he'd have concealed it around the grounds here somewhere. In that case it might take days to find, and even then how could I prove Guy Otis had left it there?

"No, the trick was to get the kid to lead me to that gun himself. When Garv here spilled the beans about suspecting you, George, I played it up for the benefit of Guy Otis, and said I was going to arrest you late tonight or early in the morning, and I threw a bluff about making you talk.

"But the point is, I never would have realized that you'd recognized young Otis, if it hadn't been for that play of yours in making him tell me he'd seen Shallcross near the Everglades Hotel at about midnight. That was overdoing it."

"Mort, you're absolutely right. I hadn't actually recognized the kid when he tried to hold me up, but I'd seen that he had on a double-breasted dinner coat, and I knew Guy Otis owned a coat like that—and the rest wasn't hard. Of course he'd seen me. So when I got a little panicky there for a while, when I thought you cops were getting too close, I called up Otis and threatened to expose him unless he amended his story in such a way as to take all possible suspicion away from the Everleigh," Vannest explained.

Morton went on: "After that I got young Otis to show me around the grounds, thinking he'd get nervous when we got close to wherever he had the gun hidden. But he didn't get nervous.

"Then Garv here discovered the bodies of those two New York crooks, and the ballistics man said the slugs taken from them had been fired from the same gun which was used to shoot Harry Shallcross' corpse. That brought me right back to the original problem of getting Guy Otis in actual possession of the gun. I remembered that he'd overheard me making a telephone date with you at ten, and I figured he might try to get in touch with you a little before that time, being afraid that if you were arrested you'd squeal on him. So instead of phoning, I went to see you personally, a little early. The last thing I expected Otis to try to do was shoot you through the window. Because, of course, he thought I was you—alone in that office at exactly ten o'clock.

"But if he was going to act that way, then I had a stunt for catching him. I called him at his house, and he wasn't in—naturally. He hadn't got back from the Everleigh yet. The servant who answered said he was out strolling, and I left the message that I'd be under the mango trees in a little while. I didn't say who I was—just told the servant Mr. Guy Otis would know that—but I framed the message in such a way that young Otis would certainly think it was from you. Which he did. And he was waiting for you. But of course, I never thought you were coming."

McGarvey cried: "Say, wait a minute! Maybe I'm a half-wit, but I still don't know who shot Harry Shallcross!"

MORTON EXPLAINED. "HE shot himself. I suspected that from the beginning, and I confirmed it when I had Jeffries, from the Floridian Laboratories, take a hot paraffin impression of the right hand of the corpse and then wash it out with diphenylamine and concentrated sulphuric acid. It showed a good strong glitter of nitrates between the thumb and first finger. But I didn't say anything about that because I didn't want the tip to get out that I suspected anybody but George."

Vannest said: "Shallcross had lost more than I told you. He was cleaned out. Of course I was the one who put the two hundred in his pants pocket. He'd dropped about two thousand the other night, which ordinarily wouldn't be much for him. He was supposed to be rich. He always had been. But it seems he was really almost wiped out. And when I invited him to walk into the office and make out a check—never suspecting anything was wrong—he knew that the check wouldn't be good. I suppose he just couldn't stand the thought of being poor. And I suppose he happened to see the little twenty-two I kept in the upper desk drawer there. Maybe the drawer was partly open, as it often is. Anyway, he got that gun and shot himself through the brain. Nobody heard it because that office is sound-proof. And a minute or so later I step in and find myself with a corpse on my hands. Well—" He shrugged. "The syndicate's put about three-quarters of a million into that shanty, which happens to include every cent I have in the world. Could I see the business ruined because of a scandal like that? I thought it over, and decided I'd rather take a risk of being arrested for murder.

"It just happened that those two tin-horns from New York came in at about that time and tried to sell me a hot car. Ordinarily I'd have laughed at them. But the other night I realized I was going to need a strange car soon, so I pretended to fall for the stunt."

He turned to Morton. "Who killed those fools, by the way?"

"Guy Otis. It seems they had an assignment from Maxie Scholtz to collect a debt from this kid. He and his uncle live in New York half the year, and I suppose the kid had got himself in a jam there, too. Maybe Scholtz was pressing him for it, by mail, which inspired him to try stick-up work. I suppose, when the two chiselers started south, Scholtz gave them the kid's name and address and asked them to see what they could do about collecting. He promised them a fifty-percent commission, according to their notebook. They came here, sold you the car, and then went to see young Otis. He didn't have any money, having lost his necker-bandit loot at roulette, but they wouldn't believe that. So they put on a little act. They tried to act like movie gangsters. Horowitz even pulled an old pistol that wouldn't work.

"They didn't realize what a crazy galoot they were talking to. He was desperate. He lost his head, whipped out his own gat, and started shooting in all directions. How he managed to get the bodies out there, I don't know. But the very fact that they were there argued a knowledge of the countryside. He couldn't have picked a better place— except for those buzzards, which he never counted on."

"I hate to think," said young McGarvey, "that buzzards ever did anybody any good, even detectives."

George Vannest smiled. "You'd hate to think that of gamblers too, wouldn't you?"

"Well, some gamblers might be all right, but I've got to admit I don't approve of gambling itself. It just isn't right," said young McGarvey. "They oughtn't to allow it."

THE SCAR CLUE

Detective Morton had enough to do trying to catch the man with the scar and find the murder loot, without his own partner, young McGarvey, butting in intent on killing his quarry. There was only one thing to do in a case like that. Lay the dumb kid cold before he gummed the works and pray that he'd never guess it was his sidekick who'd put him in a coma.

1

MURDER AT THE ST. CLAIR

IT WAS AN unimportant little hotel, and the bellhop couldn't understand English. That's why he didn't know what the men were quarreling about in 619. It frightened him a bit, and excited his curiosity; he was a singularly inquisitive little chap anyway. He kept wondering if those men were going to fight. They sounded as if they might.

There was an elevator, but the bellhop was not allowed to use it except in answering hurry calls or when he was taking guests up to their rooms. So he started down the six flights of stairs, moving slowly, wondering.

Between the third and fourth floors he paused. Had a door slammed up there? He thought of going back, and then he told himself that would be silly, but he still wondered about the sound. He vacillated. He had started down toward the third floor again, when he suddenly made up his mind. He couldn't explain afterward what it was that had caused him to go back. Just one of those crazy hunches.

The sixth-floor corridor was deserted, and strangely quiet. The bellhop approached the door of 619, now ajar. He would knock, he decided, and if the *señor* was annoyed he'd say he had got the wrong room and so sorry.

He knocked.

The door flew open. Somebody in brown—it was the best description the bellhop could give—reached out and grabbed the front of his jacket, and violently yanked him into the room. He had a flash of somebody lying on the floor, of somebody else leaning out of a window.

That was all he remembered. When he came to, he found himself stretched across a corpse sticky with blood.

He had been stunned by a blow at the base of the skull, and he was hysterical, so that it was some time before he was able to tell a coherent story. Which is one reason why the Havana police were late about getting the message to Miami.

MONTGOMERY TOOK IT in to Morton and McGarvey. Morton was already working, methodically, without haste. Captain

*Morton socked him
with the chair*

Montgomery said, "Some work for you, Mort," not exhibiting much enthusiasm.

"Not for me," Morton said. "Give it to the ape man here."

McGarvey, all six feet three of him, straightened. He turned around, lurched forward, grabbed the telegram.

"It's a murder!" he enthused, after reading it.

Morton murmured: "That's nice. You're nuts about murders, aren't you? First one you've had for some time." He didn't look up.

"It's a guy shot in Havana—an American. They want us to pick up the guy who had the hotel room where he was shot—another American. Name's Arthur Johnson. They think he powdered on the Clipper."

"Description?"

"Some. Enough, anyway."

At last, Morton began to show some interest. You never could hurry Morton, nor excite him. He looked more like a conscientious bank official than the best police detective in the state. He was gray and neat and careful and exact, and he had more brains than all the rest of the force put together. Now he glanced at his watch.

"Nice time to tell us about it. The Clipper should have landed twelve minutes ago. Give 'em a ring."

He went back to work.

Captain Montgomery grinned at the pair. They were famous. Brains and brawn. Bluster and quiet efficiency. Morton, more than twice McGarvey's age, was unsensational—but he got things done. He could fight when fighting was necessary, but he preferred less noisy methods. He seldom raised his voice. He never smiled. Habitually he rode hell out of young McGarvey, who worshiped him.

McGarvey was tough, and proud of it. He wasn't altogether dumb—he had his moments—but Morton seldom trusted him alone with anything but petty routine. He was a 230-pound bulldog. When he got excited, as he very often did, he became loud-mouthed. It was sheer nervousness. He wasn't naturally a bully. He should have been patrolling a beat. For a youngster, he was curiously old-fashioned, but he was all cop, and the son of a cop. His father, once Morton's partner and closest friend, had been killed at Morton's side in a gun battle they still talked about.

Morton and the senior McGarvey had gone into a night-club in response to a report that four suspicious characters were there. The four suspicious characters, at least three of whom turned out to have long criminal records, didn't wait for questioning. When they saw detectives coming they hauled out guns and began to blast. Old man McGarvey had gone down with enough lead in him to sink a ship. Morton himself went to the hospital; and he would limp a little for the rest of his days.

Two of the gangsters were killed. Autoposies showed that both were drug addicts. A third, badly wounded, was likewise an addict; the state of Florida carefully nursed him back to health—and then just as carefully killed him in an electric chair. The fourth man escaped, held up a physician in Hollywood, just north of Miami; and, at the point of a pistol, he had made this physician treat a wounded fore-arm. After that he disappeared.

Morton hadn't been able to attend old man McGar-vey's funeral. He wasn't even conscious at the time. When he had got out of the hospital, two months later, he found that a new partner had been wished on him—McGar-vey's hulking son, promoted from harness to the detective division. The promotion had been made on a sentimental impulse. It was like electing a senator's widow to complete the senator's unexpired term.

Morton had rather resented it, at first, complaining that young McGarvey wasn't good for anything except to get into fights; but they'd been together for almost a year now, and Morton had come to like the kid.

NOW YOUNG McGARVEY read the message carefully, mumbling the words, marking them as he went along with a large and not very clean finger. Morton kept on working, paying no attention.

"It says here that more information will follow shortly."

Morton clipped: "What more information do you want? Get the airport! Maybe the plane's late today."

McGarvey got the airport, and talked with various persons. His loud voice filled the room. It was a furiously hot day, and very quiet. The season was about over. The cars with out-of-state license plates were few now, and the hot spots were boarded up.

"It came in on time," McGarvey finally reported, "and a guy answering this description got off. No bag. Took a cab, and I had the cabby himself on the wire just now. Says he took the guy to the Ponce de Leon. Don't know whether he went in or not." He scowled at the ceiling. "Shall I call the Ponce de Leon?"

"Might be a good idea," said Morton.

Montgomery said, "I'll let you boys worry about it," and went out.

No Arthur Johnson was registered at the Ponce de Leon. Nobody answering that description. McGarvey seemed baffled.

Morton said, a shade impatiently: "Well, you'll never get anywhere just sitting here and talking over the telephone.

Why not go to the Ponce de Leon? Go out to the airport and ask questions."

"That's a good idea," young McGarvey said.

"And give me a ring now and then, and I'll tell you whether anything more's come in from Havana."

McGarvey got nothing at the hotel, and very little at the airport; but at least, Morton reflected, it took him out of the office for a little while. Besides, when he called in to report, Morton did have some more information from Havana.

"There's a detective named Gomez flying here," he told McGarvey. "I've met him before. Smart little fellow. And listen. It says they now believe, from cards and like that found in his room I suppose, that this guy Johnson is a professional gambler."

"So what do I do? I'm hungry."

"All right then, eat. But after that you chase yourself around to every place you can think of where there's any games. It won't do those boys any harm to know that we're not forgetting about them, anyway. But don't go sticking your nose into a fight! "

Morton was not notably interested in this Cuban case; but he was concerned about his partner. Young McGarvey had been idle for more than a month—no real excitement, no fights—and that was dangerous.

Miami was uncommonly quiet these days. Morton was glad of that, personally; but he knew his sidekick. Just as crazy and just as Irish as his old man, this kid was. Moreover, young McGarvey was a moralist—didn't drink, didn't gamble, and didn't like men who did.

Morton, even while he worked, was wondering whether

he should have sent the kid out like that on an inspection tour of the local chance joints. The big, well regulated places were mostly closed now. The places still open were smaller, meaner—and more dangerous.

The telephone rang. Morton answered, listened, frowned. After a time he said: "I'm busy with something here. What's the matter with Morrissy?... He did, huh? Well, tell him I'm busy. I've got a murder of my own to attend to. They get much?... Nothing at all? Well, what's the idea then? The watchman come in too soon for 'em? What floor was this on?"

When the man at the other end said it was the top floor, Morton cried: "Why, that's the Saint Clair! Closed up last week. What would anybody be doing in there?"

The man on the other end said: "Dunno. But the watchman had to take it in on his regular rounds, once every half hour. He plugs something up there, to prove he didn't miss it. Well, when he didn't plug it tonight, it automatically rang an alarm outside the building. A couple of the patrol boys went in, and went all through the place looking for somebody, and finally they found this watchman stretched out in the Saint Clair. You better come around, no kiddin', Mort."

Morton slammed the receiver back. "Do I have to take care of everything in this department?" He went out, scowling a little. It wasn't that he objected to work—it was just that he worried about young McGarvey.

MIAMI IS PROUD of the Kitchner Building. Not because it's a skyscraper—it reaches a mere eight stories—but because it's so fancy and modernistic. Its facade is stunningly beset with shiny oblongs and triangles of chromium; its lobby is bewildering, magnificent in mirrors. Most of the offices are occupied, in daytime, by doctors and dentists. The whole eighth floor, however, houses the Saint Clair Club, a high-class, reliable, almost staid, gambling establishment.

There never had been any scandal about the Saint Clair; it was decidedly respectable. It was patronized by pretty much the same people, winter after winter, and its proprietors were honest, cautious men. Just now it was closed for the season. It was locked up, and the doors were steel.

Morton found a crowd on the sidewalk in front. There was a radio patrol car, an ambulance, several uniformed men who saluted. "Sapped the watchman, from what I hear, Sergeant," one of them said. Morton went inside, went upstairs. He had to walk it, because the elevators weren't running.

Between the fifth and sixth floors he met a bored young man in white, coming down. The young man carried a small black bag.

"Dead?" Morton asked.

The bored young man answered: "Absolutely—positively."

Morton had been in the Saint Clair before, but never during the nine months of each year when the place was closed. It gave him the shivers, for a moment. The ceiling was high, the single gaming room enormous.

Morton had known the place only when it was crowded with whispering men and women in evening clothes; when liveried attendants walked soundlessly on the soft, thick carpets; when the roulette wheels were whirring gently, and the white ball was spinning; and, over in the corner, the big steel bird-cage was being tip-tilted. There never had been much noise; but always there had been lots of light—hard, white light everywhere.

Now the place was dim, packed with long, eery shadows. Either the electricity was shut off on this floor, or else nobody had been able to find the switch. The windows were shuttered with firm steel shutters. The only illumination, fitful and uncertain, was from flashlights held by one uniformed man and one detective. Also another detective was kneeling on the floor, striking match after match, and staring at the body in astonishment as though such a thing as death had never happened before on this earth.

Morton asked Morrissy: "Long ago?"

"Only a little while," the doc said. "Still warm." Morrissy was rattled. He waved his arms. "Why the hell do you suppose anybody would break into this place, Mort? It's been closed more than a week now."

"I wouldn't know," said Morton.

He looked around. Shadows on the walls and ceiling swayed and jerked as the flashlights were moved. The place seemed to be haunted by a hundred lost fortunes, a thousand muffled expressions of joy and grief and well mannered despair. The floors were bare, the walls were bare. The tables remained in position, but each was covered by a heavy white canvas sheet, and they loomed mistily and mysteriously through the dark.

"Search the building?"

"We've got it guarded front and back and side, so's nobody can get out, and I'm phoning for men to search it."

"All right. What do you want me for then?" Morton still was thinking about McGarvey. "What good can I do?"

"Well, I figured maybe you—"

"Get the place properly searched and then give me a ring. I'll be at headquarters. I'm expecting a call."

HE GOT MORE than one call. The phone bell was ringing when he reentered his office. But it was not Morrissy. Morton's face, as he listened, was impassive; but when he spoke his voice was harsh.

"Well, when you're running a place like that you got to expect a little roughhouse now and then. You're lucky we don't close you down.... What?... He did, huh?... Busted his nose, huh?... Well, Garv knows what he's doing, and I guess if he busted a guy's nose the guy had it coming. Now don't be bothering me. I'm busy.... What?... I will like hell call him off! One more crack like that out of you, Peters, and when Garv comes in I'll send him over there to bust *your* nose, too. See?"

He hung up. Immediately the phone rang again.

"Yeah?... Oh, he did?... Well, do you expect me to break down and cry?... No listen, Masterson: That kid's all right, and he's doing just what I told him to. It'll do you guys good to get mussed up a little every now and then. Teach you your place."

Again he hung up. But he was troubled. He muttered: "The damn young fool...!" He had kept his hand on the receiver, and presently he lifted it again.

"George? Listen, has young McGarvey been in tonight?... No?... Well, he probably will be. He's out looking for a mug named Johnson, and he's going a little haywire from lack of exercise, see? You know how he gets sometimes. Handle him carefully, George, and tell him to give me a ring. Or if he should catch me in, tell him I said to go easy and stop smacking people. Tell him I said to take an aspirin. That usually quiets him down."

He hung up. The phone rang. "Another?" he asked himself wearily. But this time it was the switchboard.

"Mort? You're working on that guy Havana wants, aren't you? Well, a woman just called up and said that if we want Arthur Johnson we should go to a poker game Nutsy Walsh is running in the Cynthia Apartments. Apartment Eight D, she said. Then she signed off."

"Trace it?"

"Yeah. It came from a pay phone in that drugstore at the corner of Ponce de Leon and Coral Way, out in the Gables."

"Ring the Gables and asked them to investigate it for me, will you? I'll go over and see what Nutsy has to say for himself. He's got no right to be running a game here anyway."

He looked a little tired, as he went out of headquarters. He seemed grayer, more stolid. Morton wasn't as young as he used to be. And he had a hunch that something was wrong tonight, somehow, somewhere.

2

FOUR FLUSH

THE DOOR WASN'T opened very far, and instantly it was evident that Nutsy Walsh wished he hadn't opened it at all. He was a large, soft, pale man. He was bald. He perspired a lot.

"Hello, Sergeant. Uh— Glad to see you."

"I'll bet you are. Step out here, Nutsy."

The gambler came timorously, sideways, closing the door behind him.

Morton said: "So you're running a game again?"

"No, no! You thought I was running a game, huh? No, hell no! Just tonight I just happen to have a few personal friends in—just a friendly little game, that's all. But not a real game."

Morton didn't say anything.

"No, absolutely, Sergeant. You must have got it all wrong. This is nothing but just I and a few friends, sitting around playing cards, that's all. Somebody's been kidding you if they told you that—"

Morton hit him on the left side of the chin. Walsh, big man though he was, rocked back on his heels. Then he began to cringe away. But Morton stepped forward briskly and hit him again, this time on the right side of the chin, before he could cover his face.

"I hope you haven't a long lease on this place, Nutsy, because you're not going to be here this time tomorrow night. And not anywhere else in town either. Clear?"

Walsh didn't say anything.

Morton glanced at the apartment door. "If your game's so friendly and all that, maybe I might take a look at it. I might even sit in a few hands."

"Sure! Surest thing you know, Sergeant! Glad to have you! It's just a few friends, honest. Of course, we're playing for money, but not much—just a dollar limit is all. Just among friends."

"Yeah," said Morton. And as he walked into the entrance hall he sighed: "You certainly have come down in the world, haven't you?"

There were five men. Morton never had seen any of them before, to the best of his knowledge. Or had he? He recognized Arthur Johnson promptly. Johnson answered the description in every detail, even to his clothing. Morton gave him no more apparent attention than he gave the others; but, in fact, he was doing a lot of wondering about this man.

The five players were nervous. Walsh tried to be jocular.

"This is my friend Sergeant Morton, fellas! He's the Sherlock Holmes of Florida, ha-ha-ha! If you guys are thinking of committing any murders or burglaries or anything, better not do it while Sergeant Morton's around. Hey, Sergeant?"

Morton said nothing.

"The Sergeant's going to sit in with us for a while, fellas! Sergeant, this is Hal Easter, and this is—"

Johnson he introduced as Melvin Traub, though he stumbled slightly over the name. Morton sat down, bought some chips, lighted a cigar.

"Mix you a drink, Sergeant?"

"I don't mind."

There were two reasons why he did not immediately arrest Johnson. One was that he expected young McGarvey at any moment. McGarvey would be sure to hear, in one of the places, that Nutsy Walsh was running a game again, and he would be sure to make for Walsh's then and there. People told young McGarvey things like that because they liked him, and because they had liked his father. And the kid knew that Walsh had been forbidden to gamble in Miami again. He'd be wild! If Morton weren't on hand, McGarvey might maul the pale gambler unmercifully. McGarvey was likely to lose his head under those circumstances, and he didn't know his own strength.

The other reason was that Arthur Johnson, or Melvin Traub, or whatever his real name was, was somehow familiar. Morton, being a good detective, seldom forgot a face. And now he had a suspicion—he wasn't sure but he suspected—that he had seen this Johnson man once before. He wanted to study him. It wasn't merely a matter of formal description—height, weight, color of hair and eyes, all that. It was something more elusive. Morton wished to see how Johnson moved when he was at his ease, wished to hear him talk, watch him deal. Arrested, the man would be taut and unnatural.

And there was, possibly, a third reason. Morton loved a good game of poker.

THE PLAY WENT quietly. Nobody was very reckless, nobody was sore. Morton never appeared to be paying more attention to Johnson than to the others; but actually he was studying the man all the time, and racking his memory.

"Hot in here," he said, and rolled up his sleeves.

Men are sheep. Promptly another player said, "Sure is," and rolled up his sleeves. And then Johnson rolled up his. And Morton saw that there was a scar about four inches long on Johnson's right forearm, near the wrist.

Easter, the man on Morton's right, was a little drunk, and losing badly. He leaned far over the table. His coat hung on the back of the chair in which he sat, and Morton had noticed that one pocket sagged.

"Up again," said Easter.

Morton said: "Once more."

"Again."

Morton sighed. Easter had drawn three cards.

"Up," said Morton. It was a big pot.

"Calling and up again."

"All right. This is getting monotonous. I'll see you."

Easter threw down his cards. "One, two, three ladies!"

"Mine are aces," Morton said, reaching for the chips, "all three of them."

There was a mild buzz of comment—but it ceased abruptly. Morton, who was stacking chips, looked up. Hal Easter was leaning very close to him, glaring at him with tiny bloodshot eyes. His right hand was near the right pocket of his coat, the pocket that sagged.

"So you're a cop, huh?"

Morton nodded, said, "Sure," affably, and went on stacking chips.

"I don't like cops. Never have."

Morton didn't look around. "Lots of people feel that way," he said carelessly.

"Do the cops in this town come horning in on quiet games where they're not wanted? Is that it? I suppose you come in here because you figure these guys wouldn't dare to win from you, huh? Is that the way it is?"

Johnson looked scared. For that matter, most of them at the table looked scared, and Nutsy Walsh seemed on the verge of a swoon.

Morton didn't take his hands from the table, but he turned his head to gaze at Easter in honest amazement.

"Say, are you planning to do anything?" he asked.

The right hand edged nearer to the low coat pocket. "You think maybe I wouldn't, huh?"

Morton said: "I think maybe it would be better if you didn't, that's all."

Then there was a terrible pounding on the door. Young McGarvey, no doubt. Morton shrugged, without taking his gaze from Easter's face, and said quietly: "Better see who that is, Nutsy."

Yes, it was young McGarvey. They heard him push open the door, heard Walsh's cry of alarm, heard a curse, a thud. Morton called: "Lay off, ourangouttang! I've done that already!"

McGarvey came out of the entrance hall, into the big room, and his face clearly said: "What are you doing here?" He was dumbfounded.

Morton said peevishly: "I wish you'd get out of that habit of going around hitting people. Some day it's going to get you into trouble."

"This louse has been told he can't—"

"I know I know! But you were sent out to pick up a guy, not to go pasting every fourth gambler you come across. Quiet down! Take an aspirin or something." He nodded toward Johnson. "Incidentally, there's your prisoner." Johnson rose, his fists clenched. "Was that a crack, or are you being serious?"

"Lousy act," said Morton. "They want you in Havana."

"You're crazy! I haven't been in Havana for—"

"Lousy act," Morton repeated. "You were seen getting off that plane this afternoon. We got plenty of witnesses."

Johnson subsided abruptly. McGarvey, who still couldn't understand what it was all about, frisked the man, handcuffed him. Walsh hadn't reappeared. Everybody else in the room was silent.

"Take him to headquarters, but don't book him," Morton said. "When that guy Gomez comes he'll know what to do about it."

HAL EASTER ROSE suddenly. McGarvey yelled "Hey!" and sprang around the table. Morton pushed against Easter, hard. It knocked the man over a chair, and Morton kicked the gun which never had quite got out of its holster. Easter squealed with pain. Morton kicked him again, this time in the face.

"Ordinarily," Morton said, "I'm a cop that doesn't believe in being rough. Gary here will tell you that." He gazed contemptuously around. "But when I find myself with a flock of tin-horns like this, and one of you have the nerve to reach for hardware—then I kind of get sore." He picked up the gun, pocketed it. He jerked his head toward the horizontal Hal Easter. "Take this souse along, too. Book him for anything you happen to think of. I'll be the complainant."

"But I still can't understand what you're doing here!"

"I'll explain later." To the company at large he said: "The game's over. Go home. And make sure that home isn't anywhere in Miami. Because if I should happen to see any of you around here again"—he nodded toward his partner—"I'll turn this caveman loose on you!" He called for Walsh, who came cautiously into the room. Walsh's mouth was bleeding. Morton pushed chips to the center of the table. "Twenty-one and a half. Count 'em and cough up. I bought ten in the first place. You mugs can't even play a decent game of poker."

Outside, Morton borrowed the department car. "Take 'em down in a cab," he told McGarvey. "I want to drive around a little and think about something."

"I wish you'd tell me what's on your mind, Mort. You're always so damn secretive about things."

"Maybe a little air'll do me good. I just want to try to remember something."

For a time he drove aimlessly, and very slowly. Arthur Johnson's face floated in front of him, a tantalizing vision. Somewhere he'd seen that face…. But he had reason to believe that searching the rogues' gallery would do no good; or mugging and printing Johnson and then asking Washington about it. Johnson wasn't afraid of being arrested. In fact, Morton suspected that Johnson had wanted to be arrested.

Somewhere he'd seen that face.... Somewhere for just a little while, an instant or two.... If he kept staring at Johnson he wouldn't remember. It was better driving like this, with the vision of Johnson's face in front of him.

Somewhere, for just a flash of an instant, he'd—

It came to him suddenly. And even Morton, normally Indian-like in his immobility, tightened now, and felt his hands go wet on the wheel. But he wasn't sure.

He drove fast now, drove to Biscayne Boulevard, turned north. He was remembering the time he'd gone into a nightclub with one of the swellest sidekicks and pinochle enemies any man ever had. It wasn't so long ago. He remembered four men at a table, four hard-eyed men. The guns had appeared unexpectedly, without any warning. The noise had been terrific. Old Garv, brave with the stupid and splendid bravery of a man who didn't know the meaning of fear, had charged wildly across the room, shooting all the time—had tumbled with a crash of chairs—and had not moved again.

Morton, who had dropped on one knee behind a table, chiefly remembered the glint of his own bobbing gun barrel. It was very confusing. But Morton had been no stranger to shootings. He had kept his head about him. The gun barrel was the principal thing, yes, but he remembered some other things as well.

There was the tall scowling fellow who went right over backward in his chair. There was a blond who jumped up and started running toward them—and then abruptly sat down. There was the one with the panic-stricken eyes, who simply stood there firing from the hip, aiming at nothing in particular, frozen with fear. And there was the one who had sneaked out by the side entrance. Morton hadn't seen that fellow very well. Nobody had seen him well. Just a flash, that was all—with guns bamming all over the place, and chairs and tables falling, and everybody yelling and screaming like hell. A calculating hood, this fourth man. Perhaps he hadn't been a dope, like his companions. He had slipped away unostentatiously, but blasting all the time. Blasting accurately, too.

At the autopsy they took no less than nine bullets out of poor old McGarvey's carcass, but most of these were lodged in muscles far from the vital organs. The one they'd taken from his head was the one which had killed him. And that bullet hadn't been fired from the guns the dead and captured gangsters had held. It didn't match them, ballistics experts said. That bullet had been fired by the fourth man—the man who had escaped with nothing more than a flesh wound in his forearm.

The bullet which had broken Morton's legs, too, and had sent him to the hospital, came from the fourth and missing gun.

Just a flash Morton had had of that man. He couldn't be sure. But there was a way to find out.

IN HOLLYWOOD, AN elderly physician said: "No, it was the right arm. I'm certain of that. Because he kept the pistol in his left hand all the time. Oh, I'm sure of it! I'll never forget that night as long as I live. He sat here like this, and I sat over here, and—"

"Would it have left a scar about two inches long?"

"It would have left a scar, yes. But longer than that. About four inches, I'd say."

"It was up near the elbow? You've told us all this before,

Doctor, I know, but I was in the hospital all that time, and now I want to get it straight in my own mind. Near the elbow?"

"Oh, no! It was far down. Practically the wrist."

"All right, Doctor. Thanks. It's the wrong man, I guess."

"Shame, shame." He saw Morton to the door. "I certainly hope you do catch that rascal some day."

Morton said: "I certainly hope so, too. Good night, Doctor."

There was a good reason why he had lied to the physician. Morton himself was the only man who knew who Arthur Johnson was; and what Johnson had done about a year ago—here in Miami.

The doctor was a loquacious old codger, and the one great event in his life was the time when he had bandaged a murderer's arm. He wouldn't be quiet. He couldn't be. And news like that moves rapidly.

Cop killers aren't popular in police stations, and the men at Miami headquarters had been mighty fond of old man McGarvey. There were detectives, patrolmen, too, who had sworn to kill this fellow. There was, first and most important of all, young McGarvey. That kid, all by himself, could be harder to handle than a whole lynching mob. Now that he knew what he did know, Morton wasn't going to let Havana have Arthur Johnson. But the news must be broken very gently to old man McGarvey's son. Otherwise there'd be trouble.

Morton sat at the wheel for a few minutes, staring at nothing, absent-mindedly tapping the horn but not hard enough to cause it to sound. He was very tired. It was almost midnight, and he'd been working since eight that morning. More than that, the emotional strain had worn him down. Men, who had known him for years, would swear to you that Wainwright T. Morton didn't have any emotions; but they were wrong.

Besides, he hated driving. Usually McGarvey drove the car.

But at last he started it. He went to Coral Gables, the chief there said they'd got a break. A clerk in a drugstore had remembered the woman making the call, had even remembered what she said. He knew the woman, too. A nightclub entertainer and general bum. Name was Sonia Pasha, which was undoubtedly a phony.

"Would she do anything for dough?"

"Anything, is right."

"*Umm.*" Morton was thoughtful, for a time silent. Then he asked: "Do you suppose this Sonia dame would know Nutsy Walsh?"

"Know him? Why, she used to work for him! Used to steer drunks into his dump, when he was out at the Beach."

Morton got into the car. "I wish I'd know this an hour earlier," he said grimly.

But Nutsy wasn't home. Morton got the superintendent of the apartment house to open the place for him—but there was no sign of the gambler. Hasty packing, and out. Walsh wasn't taking any chances.

Morton tried the railroad station, but the gambler wasn't there, either. He shrugged. Well, it didn't matter much. The thing was pretty clear in his mind now anyway. He drove to police headquarters.

3

THE SPANISH AMBASSADOR

YOUNG MCGARVEY, FRETFUL, puzzled, was waiting in the office. He never could understand what motivated this gray, soundless partner of his. Morton, when he worked on a case, never took anybody into his confidence, not even Montgomery.

"Well, it's this way," he consented to explain. "I got a tip by telephone that Nutsy was running a game there, and that Johnson was sitting in it, and not being able to get hold of you I went over myself."

"But what'd you play with them for?"

This fact seemed to hurt the youngster most of all. It shocked him. It didn't seem proper. But Morton shrugged.

"No harm making a little money, is there? I'd have taken in more, too, if you hadn't hurricaned in when you did."

"It wasn't just that, Mort."

"No, it wasn't. I thought I recognized the guy's face, at first. He looked like somebody I saw in a nightclub once. Your old man was with me. It was the last time," Morton said, "that your old man and I ever did go into a nightclub together."

He had wished to see how McGarvey would respond to this much information. He learned. McGarvey moved around the big desk, leaned close to his partner. His face was very red, and the backs of his hands shone with sweat.

"You mean— Listen, Mort. You mean you think this guy Johnson is the rat—is the guy that— You mean he—"

Blue veins were pounding in young McGarvey's temples; they were so very dark blue that they seemed almost black against the terrific red of his skin, and they thumped furiously. His whole face was glittering with sweat. He gasped for breath, couldn't talk.

Morton got to his feet quickly. "Now take your time, kid. It turns out I was wrong, see? He isn't the same guy at all."

"You're telling me that, Mort! You're just telling me that to prevent me from killing him! You're lying to me!"

"I'm not lying to you! Why the hell should I want to lie to an ignorant flat-foot like you? I tell you he's not the guy. I checked. That's what I went up to Hollywood for—to check with the doc who fixed his wound that night. And he's not the guy. Call the doc, if you don't believe me."

He took McGarvey's arm. McGarvey shook him off. "You're lying to me! I'll kill the rat! I'll kill the heel!" He spun around, presenting his back to Morton, who ordinarily could quiet him with a single sharp word. "And, Geez! To think I let him go!"

"You let him go?"

"Well, right after I got back here we got another wire from Havana saying they didn't have a murder charge against Johnson after all. We didn't have any charge against him here, ourselves. I didn't know how long you'd be, and I couldn't raise Monty on the phone. So I let the guy go. I was anxious to get out on this watchman murder over at the Kitchner Building."

"You half-wit! You could at least have held him for twenty-four hours as a vagrant, on general principles!"

"Well, I don't care. I'll get him anyway—tonight!" He took out his pistol. It was an ordinary police regulation .38, but he stared at it as though he'd never seen anything like it before. Morton went around in front of him, snatched the pistol.

"All right," McGarvey said. "I don't want it anyway. I'll find that guy somewhere. I don't want to shoot him anyway. I'll tear him apart with my hands!"

"Take an aspirin, Garv. Take two or three. I tell you this isn't the same guy. You can call up that doctor in Hollywood if you don't—"

McGARVEY STARTED OUT of the office. Morton got in his way. McGarvey simply pushed Morton in the chest, and Morton, though he was no small man, went staggering across the room, slammed against a wall.

"Stop that guy! *Stop him!*"

But McGarvey was gone. Morton ran outside. Too late. The department car was halfway down the block—with a madman at the wheel.

Back in headquarters, Morton raged to the switchboard man: "Get me Captain Montgomery!"

"He's at some banquet tonight, and he might be sore if—"

"Get him!"

Then Morton, himself, started to telephone. He was a born executive. All his instinct was to chase his partner, to stop young McGarvey from killing somebody or getting killed. But that was no one-man job. Morton needed all the help he could find. Meanwhile, he was telephoning to

every place where McGarvey might possibly go in search of the man who had killed his father.

When Montgomery was reached, Morton barked at him: "Young Garv's on a rampage. Don't ask me to explain now! I want every man I can possibly have. You call 'em yourself and have 'em report to me."

"You never will ask for any help on a case, Mort. You always—"

"Well, I'm asking for it now! I'm demanding it! Get busy!"

He hung up. Then he went on calling nightclubs, bars, gambling houses. He sent a message to the radio room. He was in a fever of sweat, calling, receiving calls, instructing cops—when a little man in a spotless linen suit entered the office, and bowed impeccably.

"*Señor* Morton, is it not? We have met before, I theenk?"

"Oh—Gomez. How are you? Excuse me, but my partner's gone off his pill and he's running all over town looking for your friend Johnson. He wants to kill him."

Little Gomez flashed beautiful teeth under a perfect mustache. "Who would care? It would be a good job, yes?"

"Sure, except that he might get himself killed doing it."

Gomez shrugged, smiled politely. "I had hoped," he confessed, "that you would already have Johnson in custody."

"We did have," Morton grated, "but your pals in Havana wired to let him go, and I wasn't here in headquarters at the time and my dumb partner turned him loose." He got the telegram for Gomez. "Bright, huh? Bright there, and bright here."

Bernardino de Gomez was normally the most affable of men. But now he paled with rage. He waved the cablegram.

"They are fools!" he shouted.

"Right. Here, too. Both fools, Gomez. I think you and I ought to stick around our offices after this, huh?"

"They will not wait for me! They— They are—" Too angry to talk English any longer, he broke into Spanish. He pounced upon Morton's telephone. "You call me Havana, please, and hurry, please. This is Gomez. I pay the toll. You call me Havana police headquarters. You get me Felipe Portalegre. Right now, please! This is Gomez speaking."

Morton said: "Might as well hang up for a while. They can't put through a call like that right away. Sit down. Take it easy. Somebody around here's got to keep his head tonight. Sit down and tell me who it is who's trying to put Johnson under the sod, if that's the plan."

THE LITTLE CUBAN shrugged an apology, lighted a small cigar. "I do not know their names," he confessed. "They are the Americans the boy saw in that room." He told Morton about the bellhop, about the finding of the body. "The dead man was name Petrucchio. He is American citizen. He and *Señor* Johnson, they were friends. They go many times to the Casino together. In the hotel their rooms are across the hall from the one another, see?

"This morning two men they go to Johnson's room, and Petrucchio is there but Johnson is not. They have a quarrel with Petrucchio. They shoot him, keel him. Then the boy comes in, and they hit him on the head."

"Nobody else heard this?"

"Ah, yes! We find her later. A woman in the next room. She said she hear two men yelling at another man. She understand a leetle English. She did not know all they say, but she understand some of it. They yell at Petrucchio, 'Then you know where it is! The rat he is sending you because you know where it is!' Something like that. She is not sure of the words exact."

"*Hmmm,*" said Morton. " 'You know where it is,' eh?"

"Something like that. They say it many time."

"Where was Johnson?"

"We learn later that he has been at the Pan-American office, buying one teecket to fly here to Miami. He was buying it for Petrucchio. He is coming back from the office, with the teecket, and when he gets near the hotel he hear the noise and see the crowd, and he goes straight back to the office and change the teecket into his own name, and he flies away instead of Petrucchio. He does not wait to ask questions."

"Wise guy."

"Some of this I am guessing, you understand, *Señor?*"

"Sounds straight to me. Johnson was only here a couple of hours when he started trying to get himself arrested. He got hold of a cheap gambler friend and got him to get a girl-friend to telephone us a tip that he was playing at this gambler's apartment. If he'd just walked into headquarters and given himself up, it would have looked too raw. He must have had an ironclad alibi as far as the murder of this Petrucchio went."

"Ah, yes! He was in the Pan-American office at the moment Petrucchio was murder. I learn that right away. But my so clever colleagues," Gomez added bitterly, "they must not learn it but just a leetle while ago. And so, the peegs of fools, they send this message to release him!"

" 'You know where it is,' eh?… Johnson must have been afraid to come to Miami himself, to get whatever it was he wanted, because he'd shot a cop here once. He killed my best pal. Old man McGarvey. And he put me in a hospital for two months with a busted leg."

"And he would dare to come here again!"

"He must have been desperate. When they bumped Petrucchio, he knew they were close. So he took the chance and came here himself. But why should he run such a terrible risk by getting himself arrested? He must have spotted those two hoods here, and was more afraid of them than of having me recognize him. Would those guys be here already?"

"I cannot be sure, but I theenk so. They are men of action, those two."

"They seem to be." Morton spoke into the telephone. "Get me long-distance. Barry Clair, at Saratoga Springs, New York. Yeah, everybody there knows him. Just ask the Saratoga Springs operator, tell her. And while that's going through, get me the municipal airport here. How's that Havana call coming?"

"Have it for you soon, Sergeant. Got two other trunks for you right now. Wait! here's Havana."

"Mr. Gomez will take it in Captain Montgomery's office, and give me the two local calls here."

EVERY DETECTIVE AND uniformed policeman on duty in the city that night, and some who weren't supposed to be on duty, were looking for young McGarvey. They had orders to try to quiet him, to assure him that he was seeking the wrong man, to try to persuade him to call Morton at headquarters—at least, if they couldn't make him listen to reason, they were to report to Morton where they'd seen him.

Morton took two such reports, while Gomez spoke to his native Havana in Montgomery's office. A couple of radio patrol cops had seen McGarvey far out on Flagler Street. They'd whistled him, chased him, lost him. Another pair had seen him enter a restaurant. They'd gone in after him, but he was coming out by that time. The proprietor said that McGarvey had simply stalked among the tables, glaring at every man he saw. One customer, drunk, had bumped into him, and McGarvey, without even looking at the fellow, had pushed him backward on the floor. That was all.

"If he doesn't get worse than that," muttered Morton, "it'll be all right."

From Montgomery's office came the shrill voice of Gomez, who screamed curses and recriminations. Morton sighed. He wished he could swear like that. Swearing seemed to relieve some men's feelings. It never relieved his.

The phone rang. He seized it eagerly. But it was only the municipal airport. Yes, two men had arrived in a chartered plane about two hours ago. They said they had come from the west coast. The airport authorities wished to question them, but the men had hurried into a taxi and disappeared. The pilot was still there, but he protested that he couldn't speak a word of English.

"Got somebody there who knows Spanish? He looks like a Cuban to me. Something funny about this," the man said.

Gomez came into the office, tapping his forehead with a silk handkerchief. He was smiling.

"I feel better now," he said pleasantly.

"I wish I did." Morton extended the instrument. "Here, talk to this guy. He's the pilot who brought your boy-friends, I think."

Gomez chatted for some time into the mouthpiece. He spoke sharply, harshly. Then he hung up with a crash.

"He is the same, yes. But he will not admit it. He denies he knows who those men are. He denies he brought them from Havana. He is a beeg liar, but what can we do? Shall we search for the taxicab?"

Morton shook his head gloomily. "Too late now. We've got to sit tight and see what breaks. I figured Johnson would go right out of here and bust a window, or sock a cop in the jaw, or something. But since he isn't back here by this time, I'm afraid he's not going to look very pretty when we do find him."

Gomez shrugged. "He is the better dead. The world is the better."

"Yes, but I don't want him killed in this town. Let's hope they take him for a long, long ride. And meanwhile, there's my sidekick to worry about. If he should happen to run into those two hoods, in company with Johnson, I hate to think what might happen!"

THEY SAT IN silence after that, the dapper little Cuban with his cream-and-coffee complexion, his faultless linen suit, his silky hair and mustache, and the square, stolid, tired American detective.

Gomez moved occasionally to take the little cigar from his mouth, to knock the ash carefully into a tray on the desk. Morton didn't move at all. He just sat there.

It was about one o'clock in the morning, still hot, and

the city was utterly silent. No breeze came in the open windows. The two men could hear the clock ticking in the big room outside.

The telephone bell clanged. Morton, whose hands had been resting within a few inches of the instrument, snatched it. "Hello?" He listened a moment, nodded. Presently he was talking to Barry Clair, in Saratoga Springs. Clair, during the winter, was manager and principal owner of the Saint Clair Club, Miami.

"Barry, there was a guy named Hasser, George Hasser, used to work for you here last season. I think he spun one of the wheels. Remember him? He was one of the boys, old man McGarvey and I had to puncture that night at the Green Macaw when Garv got the curtains."

Clair said: "Sure I remember him. But he wasn't working for me at the time of that shooting, Mort. I'd fired him about two weeks before that. I told you that at the time. Or at least, I told Montgomery. You were in the hospital."

"Yeah, I know. But you never did tell us why you had fired him, and I don't suppose we ever asked. I want you to tell me that now, Barry. It's important as hell."

"It really is, Mort?"

"You don't suppose I'd be spending the city's money on a call like this if it wasn't, do you?"

There was some silence. Barry Clair was a cautious man, and he liked to protect his clients and his employees alike, past or present.

At last he said: "Well, there's no secret, really. The autopsy showed him up for what he was, and the papers all carried it anyway. We fired him, Mort, because we found out that he was a user. We never caught him in anything crooked or anything, but you never can trust a user. I wouldn't have one of them working for me under any circumstances."

"Do you know whether he ever peddled the stuff?"

"I wouldn't know that. I'll tell you this, though—if he ever did peddle it, it wasn't in my place! I'm sure of that!"

"Thanks, Barry. That's all I wanted to know."

"What's up down there, anyway?"

"Oh, somebody tried to knock over the Saint Clair. Bopped the watchman. There's nothing anybody could steal in there, is there?"

"Good God, no! Not even any of the furniture. We store that. The only things we leave are the tables, themselves, and the wheels. It would almost take dynamite to get one of those wheels loose—they're set in concrete."

"That's what I thought."

"It's the craziest thing I ever heard of! What else do you know about it, Morton? Any arrests?"

"Not yet. But we ought to have it cleaned up in a few hours. Watch the papers, Barry. That's about the best I can tell you right now."

4

LEAD POISONING

AFTER MORTON HAD hung up, neither man spoke for a long time. Gomez had finished his little cigar and was lighting another, handling it delicately, like a girl handling a piece of sticky pastry. In the big room, the clock ticked relentlessly. A party of drunks drove by outside.

About eight minutes of this—it seemed like eight hours. Morton kept his hands within a few inches of the telephone, and when it rang again, crashing through the hot, still air of the office, he grabbed it.

"Is this Sergeant Morton himself?"

"Himself."

"This is Leslie, out at the Green Macaw."

"Yeah. Young McGarvey been there? Is that it?"

"Oh, no. I been watching out for young Garv, like you boys asked, but he hasn't shown up. No, this is something else." There was some silence. Then Leslie said hesitantly: "Last time I called you up about a thing like this, Sergeant, it was a little over a year ago, and it caused all sorts of trouble."

"I remember it," Morton said grimly.

"Well, let's hope this ain't any history-repeating-itself business, tonight. Maybe you think that other affair got me jittery or something. And if it comes to that, maybe it has. I don't know. Anyway, if you think I'm just making a damn fool out of myself—"

"For God's sake, stop apologizing! What is it you want?"

"Well, practically the same thing as the other time."

"Four more suspicious babies?"

"Well, only two this time. That is, three all told. But two of them look mighty bad, and the other one looks scared out of his wits. He's been trying to S.O.S. the waiter, with his eyes. The third guy, I mean. They got him between them, and they're all three sitting in that last booth, the same place those four gangsters were that time you and old man McGarvey—the time old McGarvey got— Well—"

"Go on," said Morton. "I've got control of myself now. I'm brave. I can hear the worst. How long have these guys been there?"

"About half an hour. The two on the outside certainly look like bad babies, Sergeant. I wouldn't fool you!"

Morton said: "Describe the guy in the middle."

Leslie described him. Morton squeezed his mouth shut until the lips were thin and white.

"He seems scared stiff," Leslie finished.

"He ought to be. I'm surprised to learn he's still alive at all."

"You know who they are?"

"I think so. Just don't pay any attention to them, and I'll be out there as fast as I can make it."

"There won't—there won't be any shooting this time, will there?"

"I hope not. But I wouldn't care to make any promises."

He hung up, exhaled, stared somberly at Gomez, who was examining faultless fingernails.

"Sounds like our pals. They've got Johnson out in a cheap dump out toward Hialeah. Looks like they were asking him questions kind of hard. He's lucky he's not in a back seat with them. Maybe he will be soon, if we don't get out there fast enough. I don't imagine those guys have got much patience, do you?"

"Shall we got out and get them, then, *Señor?*"

"Guess we'll have to." Morton rose slowly. "Nobody around here to send. Everybody's out looking for that crazy Irishman."

"You and I should be enough, *Señor.*"

"We should not," corrected Morton. "If you think I'm going after a pair of murderers like that without a few extra cops with me, you're mistaken! We'll take a department car and pick up some patrolmen on the way. But we'd better move fast. I don't want to be away from this office any longer than I have to."

Morton drove nervously, rather irritably, but fast. His eyes kept moving right and left.

"When you want a cop there's never one around," he muttered. "Used to make me sore to hear people say that, but now I understand."

THEY WERE WITHIN half a mile of the Green Macaw when Morton caught a glimpse of a radio patrol coming up a side street. He braked, put the car into reverse, and started back to signal these men.

Then McGarvey flashed past.

McGarvey didn't see them. He didn't see anybody. He was going at least seventy miles an hour. At that speed,

Morton wouldn't have recognized the car, but he couldn't fail to recognize the hulk of his partner behind the wheel.

Morton didn't wait for the radio patrol. He shot the car into second, into high, and went after McGarvey.

The Green Macaw, though a roadhouse, is within the city limits of Miami. However, those limits, which are nothing if not ambitious, embrace vast stretches of undeveloped land. The Green Macaw might just as well be out in the country. It is a rather dismal, year-around establishment, with a shaky dance orchestra, colored-paper streamers, and a terrible floor show.

Leslie, a long and slat-like figure of a man in dirty dinner clothes, stood near the entrance whispering with his head waiter. All the time, they were watching the three men in the far corner. They were watching particularly the two outside ones. One of these men was tallish, and had hair the color of mouldy hay. The other was thick and stolid, and a bit greasy.

When a car screeched to stop outside, the headwaiter said: "I certainly hope that's the police."

"I'm not so sure," said Leslie, and ran colorless fingers through his thin, dirty-gray hair. "Maybe it would have been better if I hadn't called, after all. Those guys really haven't done anything."

"I don't like the looks of them."

"Neither do I. But, after all, they haven't done anything wrong. Maybe it would have been better if I hadn't called."

Young McGarvey stamped in. He was like a man in a trance. The manager touched his arm, started to ask if he was from headquarters, but McGarvey shoved past him. McGarvey started to move among the tables, searching every male face. The place was moderately filled—perhaps thirty persons.

The two men in the corner did what four other gunmen had done in that same corner on a similar occasion not so long before. They saw a big cop coming and took it for granted that he meant to arrest them, and they acted first. They rose in their places, and the tall one reached under his coat. Johnson turned his head.

If the men had kept still, young McGarvey might have pushed right past them and never seen Johnson at all. But the tall fellow growled: "Yeah? And you're going to do it all alone, flatfoot?"

McGarvey's head snapped around. At a nearby table, a woman, sensing trouble, or perhaps seeing that the tall man was about to draw a pistol, let out a long, high scream.

McGarvey whirled, collided with the tall hoodlum. That fellow's right hand started from under his coat. McGarvey misinterpreted the movement, thought it was going to be a punch, and slammed his right fist into the man's abdomen. The man crashed to the floor, scattering chairs, overturning a table.

Johnson's chair, struck by one of the man's legs, tipped back. Johnson tried to cover his face with his arms—but then he was forced to flap those arms wildly in an instinctive effort to regain his balance. The chair stayed upright. But McGarvey had seen Johnson.

The smaller man stepped back, crouching. He was drawing a gun, too, but slowly, not with any show of excitement.

"So that's the way it is?" he purred.

WHEN MORTON AND little Gomez burst through the door, at this moment, McGarvey was staring wildly at

Arthur Johnson. He didn't even seem to see the other man, not four feet away.

People were diving under tables, running for the door. Morton had his gun out. He saw the smaller hoodlum aim at young McGarvey. Then a squealing woman ran into Morton full-tilt, clung to him hysterically. He tried to push her aside, to raise his gun.

Little Gomez fired twice from the hip. His long, thin, shiny revolver had appeared from nowhere, and he handled it with seeming negligence, like a man who knocks the heads off daisies with a walking stick. He stood calm, poised, even smiling a bit, his feet wide apart.

The shorter of the gangsters whirled completely around. His gun exploded as he turned. Then it fell out of his hand. He slipped to his knees, almost went flat. But he shook his head frantically, reached out with his left hand. Gomez fired again.

Now Morton was free of the crowd, and charging for the corner. The man McGarvey had knocked down was dragging himself to his knees. Gasping, snarling, he straightened his gun, a huge black automatic. Morton fired three times at him. Morton wasn't trying to do any fancy marksmanship work, like Gomez. He wasn't trying to send the gangster's gun flying with a bullet perfectly placed in the right wrist. He shot for the chest—and the chest he hit. The man with the hay-colored hair didn't move after that.

McGarvey had gone completely mad. He didn't even seem to hear the gunfire. For a long instant he stared at Arthur Johnson, on the far side of the table. Then he dived at Johnson—dived clear across the table, both arms outstretched. The two men went to the floor with a terrific crash.

The place was in a turmoil, with only Bernardino de Gomez cool and motionless and silent. Morton sprang to the corner, tossing chairs aside, hauling back the table. He kicked two guns to the far end of the room. Then he grabbed his partner by the shoulders.

Six big men couldn't have pulled McGarvey off Arthur Johnson in that terrible moment. McGarvey's enormous hands were around Johnson's throat. It was a death grip, the grip of a madman.

"Don't kill him, you ox! Don't kill him! He's got to tell us—"

There was only one thing to do. Morton liked this boisterous youngster, the son of thick, tough old McGarvey. Morton liked him a lot, and hated to smack him down. But there was no alternative.

Morton grabbed the nearest chair, swung it heavily to the base of McGarvey's skull.

McGarvey stiffened a little, blubbered something. But his grip on Johnson's throat didn't relax.

Morton swung the chair again, harder. It crashed and splintered against the same spot. Then McGarvey went limp.

Morton shook Johnson, slapped Johnson's face. Johnson's eyes rolled down a little. The man stared at Morton as though through a mist; there was no comprehension in his fixed expression. Abruptly he began to cough blood. He didn't move his head—just coughed lightly and doggedly, and blood gushed from out of his mouth as though it had been awaiting this opportunity for years.

There was nothing of sympathy or loving kindness about Wainwright T. Morton. At least, not as far as this man was concerned. He didn't understand, then, that the short hoodlum's one shot, going wild, had plowed through both of Arthur Johnson's lungs. But he did understand that Johnson was dying. He knew that from the face. He slapped Johnson again.

"Where is it? We can tear the Saint Clair to pieces, you know, if we have to. Whereabouts there is the stuff—"

The coughing stopped. Without any expression at all, seemingly without even moving his lips, Johnson spoke.

"Croupiers' wash room… in the wall… high up near the washbasin.…"

Then the coughing started again, and the flow of blood. It didn't last long. Presently, with his eyes still wide open, Arthur Johnson died. Morton rose as a couple of cops entered.

"All right, all right." He was quiet again now. "One of you call for an ambulance, and then call the morgue. Both these guys are under arrest, if they're alive. The charge is murder. I'll be in headquarters in about half an hour. Ring me there."

Gomez hadn't stirred. Morton paused a moment in front of him.

"That was the prettiest shooting I ever hope to see, Gomez."

"It is very kind indeed of you to say that, *Señor*. You will not need me for anything more tonight?"

McGarvey was recovering consciousness, was struggling to his knees. Morton nodded toward him.

"Might help me guide this ape back into the car."

"Certainly, *Señor.*"

Once out in the car McGarvey began to swear in a very loud, clear voice. He tried to get out of the car, but Morton stopped him.

"Take it easy, kid. The guy's dead."

McGarvey leaned back, was silent for a time. Then he asked slowly: "What the hell happened?"

"Lots," Morton said. "Seems four guys were running dope last year, and they had sixty thousand dollars worth of heroin on their hands. Guy named Hasser was holding it. He was working for Barry Clair, and he hid the stuff in a washroom there—maybe because he got a tip that federals were waiting for him outside. Anyway, that very night he was fired. He couldn't go back. You know how Clair is, once he's kicked anybody out.

"Trouble was, these boys had already sold the stuff to a New York syndicate, and collected in advance. They had to produce—or else. They didn't dare break into the Saint Clair while it was operating. Too well guarded. But it was near the end of the season, so they stalled the New York boys, meaning to break in after it'd closed up. But just before that happened, they got too noisy out at the Green Macaw one night. When your old man and I came along they took us for federals—and you know what happened then.

"Johnson escaped. He was afraid to show his mug in Miami again, for fear I'd recognize him. Also he had to keep out of the way of the New York boys, who were plenty sore. He laid low in Havana for a while, and there he made friends with a man named Petrucchio, and he proposi-tioned Petrucchio to come here and get the stuff just after the Saint Clair had closed for this season. He was actually buying a ticket for Petrucchio when the New Yorkers walked into his hotel room. They found Petrucchio there, and when they couldn't get anything out of him they got sore and shot him. Johnson didn't dare to stay in Havana after that, and he picked the lesser of two risks and came here. Either he didn't realize that Havana'd cable us, or else he thought he could clear out with the stuff before that cable came. He broke into the Saint Clair, started to look around, got surprised, sapped the watchman, and had to blow in a big hurry.

"By this time the gunmen had come here. Johnson either saw them, or else heard they were in town. He lost his nerve. The newspapers reported that he was wanted in Havana, and he knew he could prove that he wasn't even in the hotel when Petrucchio was killed; so he arranged to go to a nice safe jail. But you, you lummox, turned him loose! And before he could get himself arrested again, the boys grabbed him. They probably drove him around for a while, asking questions, and then went to the Green Macaw to get something to eat—and to ask more questions. They didn't want to kill him right away. Wanted to find out first where that heroin was. Well, maybe they did find out—but so did we."

He braked the car in front of the McGarvey residence.

"But who," Garv asked slowly, as he climbed out, "cracked down on me?"

"Guess a chandelier must have fallen on you. Or maybe it was the ceiling. Now don't wake up your mother, when you go in. Try and act like something besides a drunken elephant, for once! Take an aspirin, and blow yourself to a long sleep. You need it, night, kid."